Laughing Pig

PETER REGENT

Laughing Pig
and Other Stories

With drawings by the author

Robin Clark Ltd.
London

First published in 1984 by Robin Clark Ltd.
A member of the Namara Group
27/29 Goodge Street, London W1P 1FD

British Library Cataloguing in Publication Data

Regent, Peter
Laughing pig.
I. Title
823'.914 [F]   PR6068.E/

ISBN 0-86072-079-9

Typeset by MC Typeset, Chatham, Kent
Printed and bound in Great Britain
by Mackays of Chatham Ltd, Kent

Contents

Laughing Pig

George Gaskin's porkbutcher's shop stood just off the High
Street, with his name in gold lettering at the top. It had a striped
awning that could be let down in summer and a plate-glass
window in which George kept a large pot of basil, usually
surrounded by a display of chops and pork-cheeses. In winter
there would be legs of pork, swags of sausages and even whole
pigs on display, but in the hot weather the meat and sausages
were banished from the window, which was then occupied by a
family of pottery pigs. There was Father pig, about a foot high,
wearing a butcher's apron; Mother pig, slightly smaller, in a
mother-hubbard dress; Master Pig, in a sailor suit, and Miss Pig
in a skirt with bloomers showing from underneath.

Inside, the shop was spotless, with clean sawdust on the
wooden floor and a smell of basil and fresh sausages. Those
sausages were not the sad grey affairs that one finds wrapped in
cellophane, nor were they blotchy limp fingers, stippled
shocking pink on a livid ground, like those offered by the family
butcher further down the High Street. George Gaskin's
sausages were plump, sleekly glistening and rosy; in the pan
they swelled and browned, exuding just the right amount of fat,
and bursting with the utmost discretion to provide an accent of
crispness to set off their rich, moist insides.

The sausages were outstanding, and people coming in from
the surrounding country areas would be sure to take back a
supply. But the pies were superb. Mrs Gaskin made them
herself, cutting up the meat, lightly roasting it, making the
pastry, forming and filling it, and finally baking the pies in a
great flurry of activity that ended only in the early hours of
Wednesday, so that the pies were ready for market-day. Mrs
Gaskin came into the shop on Wednesday morning to serve her

1

regular customers. People watched eagerly as she selected each magnificent tower of brown crust, brought it to the counter and wrapped it. The mingled smells of crust and meat were delicious. One could tell from the weight of the package that Mrs Gaskin carefully placed in one's outstretched hands that the pie was filled right to the top. There were always compliments:

'I think last week's pie was even better than usual!'

Mrs Gaskin would smile confidently.

'It's the meat. I always put in the best meat – from all the pig. You get a bit of leg and a bit of loin and a bit of everything. You can't go wrong with that.'

'No indeed, Mrs Gaskin, I'm sure you can't. Your pies are superb,' they said.

'Besides, it's all roasted first,' Mrs Gaskin would explain. 'Most people don't do that, but I always do. That's the secret of the flavour.'

'Ah, you have the secret, Mrs Gaskin,' they said.

'Oh yes, simply splendid!' the Vicar would add, carefully putting his pie into his shopping bag.

The Gaskins had one child, a son called William. He was quiet and cheerful, like his parents, but not particularly keen on porkbutchery. He would have liked to have been a farmer, or better still, an engineer, working with the new machinery that was just starting to appear on the farms at that time. He was highly regarded by the local boys as a motorcycle mechanic, and it was acknowledged that if Bill Gaskin couldn't get a tractor or a car to start then no one could. He liked contriving and inventing things, and he sometimes produced gadgets to help in the work of the shop, or the piemaking, but his parents were conservative and preferred the old ways, so he spent most of his spare time in a shed where he kept a lathe, making working models of engines and farm implements.

Not that he had much spare time because, like it or not, he was not to be a farmer or an engineer, but to take over the shop. It was not so much that his parents insisted very hard, but rather that he acquiesced fairly easily, knowing how much they wanted him to continue the business. It was not in the nature of the Gaskins to insist or protest very hard about anything. They were nice, obliging, industrious people.

To help with the pies Mrs Gaskin had Brenda, a brisk, buxom girl with fair hair, a rosy pink mouth and rosy pink nipples to match – as William discovered when he acquiesced in his parents' wishes and married her. Brenda was brisk and efficient at everything, from lovemaking to bathing Sandra, the daughter that arrived in due course. She was especially good at the pies, and got on well with Mrs Gaskin, relieving her of some of the heavier work as she got older. Brenda was even able to persuade her mother-in-law to use some of William's gadgets to make the work easier. They were all the more welcome because the demand for pies was growing and really quite hard to keep pace with.

'I was thinking, William. That overhead trackway you were talking about. If you made it so the pig could be hooked on as soon as it was killed we could pull it over the drain for bleeding, then over the tub for the offal, then let it down for the scalding and . . . '

William grunted as he chewed his bacon and considered. Yes, he could do better than that. He could make it so that they needn't get the pig down at all; just rail it from stage to stage – even have a man set to do the first jobs and leave it to Mrs Gaskin and Brenda to deal with the experts' work.

In fact Mrs Gaskin took less and less part in the piemaking, now that it was in good hands, since she had become rather stout and her ankles tended to swell up. Brenda soon managed it all, keeping to the old lady's rule of 'meat from all the pig', and never changing the recipe for the crust, even though the mixing was done by machine. By the time old Mrs Gaskin retired the pies were made three times a week instead of once, and consignments were delivered to 'superior grocers' in all the neighbouring towns. Some were even railed to London, to the most distinguished food-hall in the land, and William bought a motor-van.

But Brenda was a stickler for quality. The pies were as good as ever. The meat was still roasted first, though William, in consultation with an oven manufacturer, had devised an oven that allowed whole pigs to pass through, still hanging from their heels from the track, being roasted as they went.

Brenda was good at publicity, too. 'Gaskin's celebrated pies' was a phrase that old Mr Gaskin liked, and Brenda had it printed in crisp, dignified blue lettering round the top of the pie-wrapping. 'All the pig goes in Gaskin's pies' was quite effective, but Brenda decided that 'The best of the pig's in Gaskin's pies' was better. She had a commercial artist design a happy pig's face that could be printed on their stationery and painted on the van. The chubby, smiling face also appeared on the pie wrapping, surrounded by 'Gaskin's celebrated pies: the best of the pig'. Soon they had two vans, and baked pies every day.

After a year or so Brenda become dissatisfied with the pig's face trademark. She stood in the grocer's and looked at the bright packets with their pictures of dancing sailors and marching chickens, and the jars of honey that were busy with grinning bees. She remembered old Mr Gaskin's pottery pigs.

Eventually, after a series of mysterious visits to town, she unveiled her idea to William. There was a whole portfolio of designs. The smiling pig's head had become an entire pig – or rather, an entire family of pigs, all with plump round bottoms and apple-cheeked, smiling faces. The drawings showed pigs running on their hind legs, napkins over their front trotters, holding pies on high like German waiters. Pigs offered pies, their eyes creased with mirth, their faces split with toothless grins. Pigs ran off with pies, grinning and looking archly over their shoulders. There were pigs in chefs' hats and pigs in sailor hats bearing the legend 'Gaskin's' or 'Laughing Pig'. Gaskin's 'Celebrated Pork Pies' were to become Gaskin's 'Laughing Pig' pies.

William was uncertain. The bright new designs lacked the dignity of the old crisply printed greaseproof. He shuffled and snorted and said he didn't know. In the end, as usual, he agreed, only standing out against Brenda's idea of showing the pigs as actually cooking pies. That didn't seem right, somehow, but the rest of it – well, Brenda probably knew best.

And it seemed that she did. Soon they needed a bigger workforce and a fleet of vans. The war came, and difficult times for the food industry, but Gaskin's was given contracts that enabled it to survive, and even to continue producing some pies of the old quality for naval barracks and the officers' messes scattered over Salisbury Plain. Then, shortly after rationing came to an end, William pressed the switch that started a new continuous flow plant. Pigs, fresh-killed and still twitching, were hung up by their heels to go swaying along in line. They were stripped of their bristles and most of their outer skin, disembowelled, scalded, roasted and defleshed almost without human intervention. It was extremely ingenious and fast yet, since every stage of the process had passed Brenda's scrutiny, the post-war product could be presented as 'unchanged – the authentic, best-of-the-pig, pre-roasted, Gaskin's "Laughing Pig" pork pie', and under each bright label with its capering pigs, Brenda took care to see that there should appear, in small but dignified print, the message: 'Gaskin's "Laughing Pig" pies are still made to the original recipe of Gaskin's Celebrated Pork Pies by the original Gaskin family'. That reassured the older customers, she said. It also pleased William.

The old shop became 'the home of Gaskin's "Happy Pig" pork pies' and sold nothing else. William was kept busy seeing that the machinery of the bakery – he refused to call it a factory – was properly maintained, and he was always devising improvements. But as the system became more and more perfect it needed less of his attention, and he spent more time on the pig-farm that had been established to provide a steady supply of pigs for the pies, and went some way towards realizing his earliest ambition.

Brenda, too, had brought the piemaking to such a peak that she no longer spent all day at the bakery, though she still walked round each morning in a white coat. If everything was in order – and it usually was – she moved on to the office, where she inspected the books, or perhaps discussed a new campaign of Happy Pig advertising with the man from the agency. In the afternoons she liked to go out. She loved trying on clothes. William had to change from his overalls to drive her into the town, and he was sent off to buy what Brenda called 'bits and pieces' for his workshop while she visited the boutiques. She tried on more than she bought, but she always came away with something, and would discuss her purchases and the problems of the business on the way home.

'I think that coffee-coloured blouse will be just right for my jersey suit. By the way, William, I'm not happy about the liver pâté. It smells the shop out, and it's not going all that well.'

William would grunt.

'I need some more shoes, though – pale, to go with my spring coat. No William, I think we should drop the liver pâté altogether. Can't you manage something?'

The pigs' livers were the last technical problem. The machinery now scraped and flayed the carcases, eventually cooked them and stripped the roast meat from the bones, which were ground up for fertilizer. But the machines could not deal with the insides of the animals, since the waste offal – which was chopped up and eventually sent to the pig-farm to feed the rising generation – had to be separated from the usable parts: the fry, the kidneys and the liver.

'I reckon we could present the carcase to a machine that would gut it,' said William. 'And we could arrange for the kidney to be taken out separately at the second operation, because the kidneys are at the back, you see. You'll want the kidney for the pies, of course. But the liver would have to go for pigfeed along with the rest. It wouldn't be wasted because it would enrich the feed and we could add more meal and cut out the oil – might improve the flavour of the meat.'

'Well, I must leave that to you,' said Brenda. 'All I know is I'm not keen on the pâté – it's more trouble than it's worth, and there's too much liver to get rid of it any other way.'

'Never liked liver pâté much myself,' said William. 'Foreign sort of stuff.'

And so the piemaking became still more automatic, with whole pigs entering on the line at one end and a trail of glistening roast pork rolling out at the other, and bonemeal and liver-enriched pigfood emerging at different stages of the process. Now the human participation was confined to actually killing the pigs and hanging them on the line, and to forming and filling the crusts for the pies. Brenda insisted that the pies must still be formed by hand, although it would have been simple to make that stage automatic too.

'It wouldn't be the same,' she said. 'Laughing Pig pies are just as good as Gaskin's celebrated pies, or better – and you can't beat a hand-formed crust.'

The new wholly automatic process became famous. People came from abroad to admire it. The report of the Common Market inspectors was pinned up in Brenda's office.

'The prime meat content of Gaskin's Laughing Pig pies is above average,' it said. 'And the efficiency and hygiene of the meat processing plant is quite outstanding and well above the minimum EEC requirements. We believe it is unlikely to be surpassed in the foreseeable future. These pies may be sold throughout the EEC without restriction.'

William was rather pleased with the 'unlikely to be surpassed' bit, but of course, such definitive success left him with even less to do in the bakery. He spent still more time at the pig-farm and was sorry when Brenda's shopping expeditions took him away and even more resentful when she decided they must start taking holidays abroad.

'Nasty place!' he said, on the Riviera. 'Food all messed about – and not a pie to be had.'

'Of course there is,' said Brenda. 'There's our own. We fly them here twice weekly.'

'Not as fresh as at home,' grumbled William.

.'Now that's just where you're wrong!' stated Brenda, whose quality control extended to point-of-sale, no matter how remote it was. 'A Laughing Pig pie in Monte Carlo is as fresh as a Laughing Pig pie in our own shop. *And* it's only been chilled – never frozen!'

'Hmph!' said William. 'They don't taste the same, anyway.'

'Well, it must be you,' said Brenda. 'Probably the climate – makes things taste different, I suppose. Oh, I am getting the sun, look. You'll have to put some stuff on me.'

She got up from the sand on to her neat pink feet, and her plump tapering hams swayed not ungracefully as she picked her way to her beach basket. William rubbed sun-oil into her back. Amazing how long people seemed between the top and bottom halves of a bikini! Sandra was the same. She had her mother's small feet, too.

'Ooh, scratch me just there, William,' said Brenda. William

scratched, and thought of his pigs.

Sandra came running out of the sea in her bikini. She was nearly twenty-one now, and her pink torso and legs curved plumply into her skimpy costume. Other people on the beach wore even less than she did. Some, a little way off, followed the new continental fashion of wearing nothing at all. As they lay in the sun, their long brown bodies bleached by the intensity of the light, they reminded William of the Laughing Pigs – especially the women, with their plump thighs and round bottoms. He sighed, and wondered how the pigs were getting on.

When they got back everything was running perfectly as usual. Brenda plunged into the preparations for Sandra's twenty-first birthday party, and no sooner was that over than a wedding was announced. Shopping expeditions became more frequent and longer than ever; Brenda helped Sandra choose her trousseau and bought nearly as much for herself. For a brief period, recently, the two of them had been the same size, and Brenda had enjoyed trying on Sandra's things. Now Sandra had lost her puppy-fat and Brenda had become stouter, so she bought her own shortie nightdress, like Sandra's, but coffee-coloured instead of white. She considered coffee a rather sophisticated colour.

William surprised the nightdress from behind. Brenda was standing on tiptoe, small pink heels in the air, reaching into the wardrobe, and from the frilly garment there emerged her plump bottom and chubby thighs. She found what she was looking for – a pair of high-heeled sandals – and trotted across the room laughing at him over her shoulder.

'Like it?' she asked.

The resemblance to one of the Laughing Pigs was remarkable. Brenda giggled at his bewildered look, and there was the resemblance again. She twirled to show off the nightdress and William saw little trotters neatly twinkling and plump thighs swaying. It was quite disconcerting.

And again, a few days later, William passed by the open door of Sandra's room when the wedding dress was at last being tried on. Sandra's head and shoulders were invisible in a mass of cascading white satin, but below, slowly disappearing into the frothy whiteness, her neat rump wriggled in diminutive pants like the rear end of a porker with a slate-blue stripe wriggling to get under a gate – or like a Laughing Piglet at the seaside. Sandra's head appeared at last, chubbily laughing; cheeks plumped up beneath her eyes.

'It's too tight, Mum,' she wailed.

William turned away, and went to look at the pigs. Halfway there he changed his mind, and went to the bakery instead. He still looked in several times a week at odd moments. He liked to keep in touch, and chat to the few human beings who tended the machinery, but more particularly, he liked to see that the machinery was working properly. Even now he kept an eye open for possible adjustments and improvements.

He passed the area where the pigs were unloaded, raising a hand to the men. He climbed on to the gangway that ran through the plant, and moved away from the screams of the dying animals and into the din of the machinery. The carcases came clattering up from the despatcher, each one hanging by the heels from his patent locking hook that could turn its burden and present it at just the right angle to the scarifier, the opening knife, the disemboweller, the kidney-seeking device and so on.

The great pink bodies loomed past him, one on every second or third hook. They swung out over a vat of boiling water and, one after the other, were plunged in, held under for two minutes, then heaved out, streaming and steaming, to be received by the scarifiers that wrapped them in flailing steel brushes. William looked at them in the steam. They were like Laughing Pigs at bathtime – though he had to admit that the big one really was more like Brenda . . . He twisted his head to see the upturned body the right way up, just as the steam and froth of the vat welled up over it, like the frothy coffee-coloured nightdress descending over Brenda's body. It suddenly struck him as funny – Brenda and her Laughing Pigs – no wonder she was so clever with them! And Sandra a little porker too!

He laughed and choked from laughing upside down in the steam. He righted himself, but felt momentarily dizzy and, still chuckling, put out a hand to steady himself. His hand found a convenient purchase, and he grasped it.

In fact he had seized one of the hooks that happened to be

empty. He realized at once and let go, but the patent locking device had already come across and trapped his hand. He put the other hand up to open the lock just as he was jerked up, off the platform, and carried along between two pigs. Absurdly, it struck him that the one in front looked like Brenda, and as the patent hook rotated he discovered that the one behind looked like Sandra. He kicked out trying to reach the railings of the gangway, but the hook dragged him away and by now the fingers of his left hand were trapped as well. He was already entering the steam and, realizing his danger, he shouted at the top of his voice.

The men loading the pigs on to the hooks heard what sounded like a cry from the processor, but took it for the clanking of machinery. A few seconds later they distinctly heard a much shriller sound: a shriek, suddenly cut off. One of them grinned at the other.

'Sounds like another one went through,' he said.

The speed of the work was such that pigs were sometimes loaded on to the line before they were quite dead, their struggles going unnoticed among the death-twitches of their neighbours. Sometimes they recovered enough to squeal as they ground towards the vats, but there was no point in running to despatch them because they had invariably been plunged into the water before one reached them, and their death, if unpleasant to think about, was pretty well instantaneous.

At the other end of the conveyor the belt of shredded and roasted meat emerged without pause. William's clothes had been removed by the machine that took off the bristles and the outer layer of pigskin. The rags and mangled leather had been chopped up with bowels and hearts and livers and mixed into the pigmeal. His battered watch would present no difficulty to jaws that sometimes chewed concrete to relieve monotony. His bones were already in the bonemeal hopper.

His disappearance was a complete mystery. He had last been seen in the bakery yard, but it was quite usual for him to go from the bakery straight to the pig-farm. Brenda admitted that he had been a bit odd recently, looking at her and Sandra in a funny way. She thought he might be upset about Sandra getting married – after all, she was an only child. Perhaps he just wanted to be by himself for a bit, though he might have said something to stop people worrying. Brenda felt sure he wasn't far away, and she had an idea he would turn up on the day – probably just appear at the reception as if he'd never been away. He certainly wouldn't want to miss that, if only because of the pies.

So preparations for the wedding went ahead without William, who in any case always left that sort of thing to Brenda. On the day the church was full, the ringers pulled away at the back and the weather was flawless. A hundred people sat down to prawn cocktail and outsize Happy Pig pies served with salads. Sandra was extremely proud and fond of the family product, and Brenda said it was a good advertisement. The guests were unanimous that the pies were more magnificent than ever.

But William did not come. Nor did he return after Sandra had left for her honeymoon. Brenda was at a loss to explain it. She'd been a good wife to him all these years . . .

But she was not one to brood, and in her brisk way she went back to the business of the bakery – and to her shopping. She arranged for one of the vanmen to drive her and found it rather convenient to know that William wasn't waiting as she tried on hats. She told the driver he could bring his wife and the two of them shopped together, the wife admiring Brenda's purchases and usually returning home with something that Brenda just couldn't resist, even though she couldn't wear it herself.

At the bakery a couple of weeks after the wedding Brenda was in the middle of arranging a series of Laughing Pig advertisements to be shown on television. The designer had brought a series of drawings for her approval and they were scattered all over her desk. The pigs capered before her eyes, some offering pies or carrying baskets of them as usual, but some dressed as Superpigs, sustained by pies and zooming about, and others setting off in spacesuits to deliver Laughing Pig pies to the outer galaxies. As Brenda studied them, eyes narrowed and lips pursed, the manager of the processor came in, unusually diffident.

'I thought you ought to know,' he said. 'It's not much, really, but I was just talking to old Tom – you know, the one that cleans up in the processor – it seems he saw William that day, and no one thought to ask him because he's only a casual.'

'Well, the others saw him too,' said Brenda.

'Yes, but this was a bit later, on the catwalk, and it was a bit odd . . . '

'Didn't he look all right?' Brenda was sure that William had lost his memory, or something of the sort.

'Oh, he was all right, but . . . well, Tom says he was laughing.'

'Well, why shouldn't he be laughing? He liked a laugh, sometimes.'

The manager was embarrassed. He laughed, too.

'Well – you know old Tom, he says funny things. He said – well, he said William was laughing like a – he said he looked just like one of those laughing pigs!' The manager immediately felt he shouldn't have told Brenda that. 'It's nothing, I suppose. Tom's a bit quaint – it's only that he seems to have seen William after anyone else did.'

'Well, after all this laughing what did William do?' asked Brenda impatiently.

'That's it,' said the manager. 'Tom doesn't know. He thought William was laughing at him, so he took his broom and went off, and when he came back William was gone.'

'Gone?'

'He'd probably gone down to the farm by the pigmeal track – he often does that.' The manager stood wondering if he had been indiscreet. 'I just thought I ought to mention it,' he said.

'I suppose so,' said Brenda.

'I'll be going then.'

'All right. Thanks.'

Brenda looked at the drawings in front of her. They all looked a bit like William – even that one, wriggling upside down. She looked at it, and remembered the pigs hanging on the track in the processor. The processor! The upside-down pig laughed with William's face.

'Oh no!' she breathed.

Her till-keeper's mind, adept at figures, rapidly calculated dates: the special batch for the wedding – the unusually good pies!

'Oh Lord!' she made a short intake of breath, almost a snort, that turned into a sobbing, grunting sound. Her mouth opened wider, its ends curling upwards; tears welled in her eyes and she laughed hysterically.

The manager, passing the window on his way from her office, heard the sound and looked in. He stopped and stared at her sitting there, plump in that girlish dress, her eyes creased into slits, her mouth gaping, laughing and laughing. It wasn't just that she was laughing; he stared because she looked exactly like a Laughing Pig.

Great Pan is Dead!

Though he had tried to see the town as a likeness of its patron saint, stretched on the gridiron of his martyrdom, he had to admit that it was more like a reclining woman curled between the olive groves and the sea. If the castle were her head, raised and looking vacantly at the horizon, the cluster of shops and restaurants was her belly and the road curving behind the houses her spine. Suburban legs sprawled, one along the coast and the other in the hills, with villas for toes. Between her breasts lay the harbour and her long sandy lap was the town beach that encircled the bay. There, stout matrons oiled husbands, beach-boys stretched side by side in sulky groups and exchanged lies about foreign girls; children tottered before fascinated parents and the occasional self-conscious beauty bore her swaying body like a precious vase towards the water. It was a small, unfashionable place.

The Reverend John Beresford-Evans sipped gassy continental beer, crossed the bare legs that could still carry him a hundred yards at a quite creditable speed, and observed his fellow-tourists as they passed between his table and the low beach wall. Though international, they looked to him like a succession of typical congregations gone on holiday. There was the occasional pretty girl, still pink in her untried bikini, with a dark Adonis closing on her fast, but for the most part they were past their prime, in garish clothes and unsuitable hats. Beresford-Evans looked mildly on them – even on the young men, remembering that twenty years ago he had inspired his wife to exclaim in the Greek room of the Ashmolean that the athletes on the black-figure vases had thighs just like his.

He often thought of his wife. He had known her for so long –

he had been an ordinand flirting with Rome when they had met and she had laughed him out of the obsession with copes and chasubles that she always referred to as the 'Church Millinery'. She was a sturdy girl, promising well as a bearer of muscular Christians and a support in his pastoral duties. She might have been made for treading the bruised grass of garden fêtes, inspiring people to bowl for pigs and buy white elephants; no one could have been better adapted to leading the women of England – or, at least, of the parish – in the making of marmalade to the strains of Blake's 'Jerusalem'. But she was dead.

Suddenly, gratuitously, in the first year of their marriage, she had been stricken with the disease that had drained her life for eighteen years, until one day she had smiled ruefully past him at the window where the sun still shone and the birds sang in their ignorance, and died. That was a fortnight ago.

Everyone had said he needed a break and he hadn't denied it. But he would not go to Italy because it contained Venice, where he and Sylvia had wandered through narrow lanes on their honeymoon, deliberately delaying their return to the unbelievably legitimate joys of their room and its big black bed. He would not go to France, where he had taken her to be pale but cheerful on leafy promenades. He would not go to the mountains, where she had lain, well-wrapped, on terraces and put aside her book with a smile to greet his booted return. So he had accepted the invitation of an old friend who was chaplain to the dwindling Anglican community of this Greek island, where everything was unfamiliar except the language which, though it sounded strange, was always flashing reminders of theology and his schooldays.

It had been nice of Corbishley to ask him, but Beresford-Evans had found the succession of visitors and introductions and occasions for protesting 'No, I really don't mind talking about it at all' rather wearing. The imminent arrival of another touring yachtful had provided him with an excuse for moving out for a few days, and he had come here. By now he had strolled up most of the paths through the olives and inspected the dilapidated chapels at the end of them. He had visited the castle, and he had spent Sunday morning with his backside hitched in a miserere on the men's side of the church. After that there was nothing for it but to frequent beaches for the first time since he had been a curate running a windy scout camp at Cromer.

It made a change. But today, after he had looked at the sea and observed yet again the green transparency that revealed the spread limbs of swimmers, and the mobile opacities that did not quite reflect the sky, Beresford-Evans turned away bored. He crossed the two streets that made up the width of the town, and took a path up through the olives that he had not explored before. The blinding sun of nearly noon was mitigated by the trees, but when he looked back through the glaucous leaves the sea still glinted below, and the sound of the cicadas welled about him in an almost deafening intensity. He climbed on, gently perspiring, until he reached the deeper shade of a lemon grove, where the fruit hung like yellow lanterns in the green gloom overhead.

He was on the point of reaching to pick one through a gap in the net that was stretched above the path when he suddenly became aware of the silence. It was as if the cicadas had been switched off. The effect was eerie; he felt an absurd impulse to hurry away, and at the sound of hoofbeats approaching from above he felt his chest tighten so that he could hardly breathe. But when the leaves parted it was only the great, preoccupied head of a donkey that came nodding into view, followed immediately by the sideways figure of the young man who was riding on its back.

'*Herete!*' said the young man, smiling. He looked slyly from the corner of his eye, almost as if he knew Beresford-Evans's foolishness.

'*Herete!*' Beresford-Evans pulled himself together and returned the greeting. He hesitated, then turned and followed the donkey and its rider down the winding path, where they soon jogged out of sight between the trees.

By the time he reached the main promenade he was late for lunch. The waiters were no longer accosting people and inviting them to sit down, for all the tables were full and they were running back and forth, hopelessly behind with orders. Since there was no chance of eating for a while, Beresford-Evans went to look for postcards. There was not much choice: a view of the harbour, another of the castle, several of spectacular places that must be a long way off, a rack of expensive 'art' cards, and something that appeared to be local archaeology, at least – he peered at several views of a statuette flourishing an enormous phallus.

'What on earth . . . ?' Beresford-Evans bent to decipher the inscription.

'Surely you recognize the Great God Pan?'

The amused voice could have been his wife's except that hers was never quite so boyish, even before it was thinned by the years of suffering. For a moment, as he looked up from the postcard and saw a slight form in jeans and a tied-up shirt, he thought the speaker was in fact a boy. But the fineness of the hand that was raised in sudden shyness to brush away hair that wasn't really in the way – that was assuredly feminine.

'Hardly a great god, would you say?' Beresford-Evans smiled to signal that the remark was lighthearted.

'I think he is quite powerful,' said the girl, smiling back. She spoke deliberately, and now he detected a slight Greek accent.

He looked back at the cards, which were of a Hellenistic bronze that had been dug up nearby. 'I've always thought of Pan as a sort of wood-spirit playing the flute and getting up to no good,' he said. 'A sort of Robin Goodfellow chap – you know, like Puck' – but of course, being Greek she wouldn't know, would she? He added rather lamely: 'That's hardly a great god, you know,' and was surprised to find himself babbling on like this. He should have laughed and brushed it off – though the girl seemed quite amused.

'I understand,' she said.

'Anyway, Pan's dead,' said Beresford-Evans, and laughed at having dismissed the little blighter.

'Why do you say that?'

Beresford-Evans mentally kicked himself. It was too silly a conversation. 'Well, he's the only Olympian whose death was officially announced,' he said, rather heavily. 'It's in Pliny, I think. At the moment of the crucifixion, in these very waters, a voice was heard to announce – '

'It was in Plutarch,' said the girl. 'But he got it wrong.'

'Oh,' said Beresford-Evans.

'But you are right too,' said the girl. 'Pan is a country fellow – he was never an Olympian at all.'

Beresford-Evans perceived the further correction – 'never an Olympian' – lurking in the agreement. The girl was sharp. She reminded him of Sylvia in the mood for debunking candles and incense.

'But you are hungry and I am keeping you,' she was saying.

She *was* sharp! Beresford-Evans realized that she had caught him looking over her shoulder to where a waiter was clearing a table that had just been vacated. He laughed in embarrassment.

'Would you care to join me?' It didn't seem odd to ask her; she seemed more like a public schoolboy stuffed with the classics than an unknown foreign girl. All the same, he was a little surprised when she said 'All right', and walked with him to the table. But she would accept only a drink, and immediately resumed:

'You see, Thamus the sailor thought he heard a voice calling "Thamus, Great Pan is dead!" – that's what Plutarch says. But in fact he probably heard some drunken bum' – she pronounced it 'bomb' – 'shouting the ritual lament of the maenads: "Tamuz the all-great" – we say "pan-great" – "is dead".'

Beresford-Evans was impressed. 'Hm!' he said. But his companion careered off to chatter like any other young girl about her views on the town and its inhabitants. When she had finished her wine she stood up to go, and as she did so she wagged a forefinger at him and pouted her lips in a grotesquely deep-voiced warning:

'Beware the Great God Pan – he makes *mischief*!'

What an extraordinary girl!

Because it was such a small place it was inevitable that one met people again. But Beresford-Evans was nonplussed at first when a young woman greeted him as he came up the beach from his swim the next day. She was wearing a bright cloth wrapped round her hips to make a long skirt, and smiling at him from under her hair as she did up her bra – with a twinge of disappointment Beresford-Evans, who did not see why the symbols of charity should necessarily be hidden, realized that a moment before she had been bare-breasted.

To make amends for not recognizing her at once, he stopped and spoke.

'Lovely day,' he said.

'Of course. Did you enjoy your swim?' Again the evocation of his wife in that boyish voice.

'Very nice, thanks.'

'Have you cut your foot?'

Embarrassed, Beresford-Evans acknowledged the trail of blood on the pebbles – but it was all right, really . . .

In fact the plaster that the girl insisted on fetching from her basket was quite welcome. As she smoothed it on to his sole he explained that he had slipped on the rocks across the bay.

'That's quite a long swim.'

'It gives one an appetite.'

The offer of lunch was immediate, but Beresford-Evans politely declined.

'It's only a picnic and I have enough for two – I was expecting someone who has not come, so it will be wasted if you do not join me, but you must please yourself.'

It would have been churlish to refuse. Besides, he was getting tired of souvlakis and moussakas and the oily stuffed tomatoes and aubergines offered by the restaurants along the front.

The girl picked up her basket and led the way. At the sea wall she gathered her skirt and was gracefully agile. Beresford-Evans scrambed up more clumsily and followed her to a little rocky terrace in the shade of some trees. She spread bread, cheese, salads and olives on a small cloth; there was a bottle of retsina, too. Beresford-Evans enjoyed the fresh taste of the food and even the turpentine tang of the wine – it was all right, in the open air. He felt a trifle elated, though whether it was the retsina, the light perfume that hung about his companion, or the pleasure of exploring a young mind – he had always been considered very good with young people – he was not sure.

They talked about nothing in particular; about their preferences in food and scenery, and the various features of the neighbourhood. When Beresford-Evans asked about the chapel on the skyline the girl made gentle fun of the local clergy, who puffed up the hill each year to take the icons on a ceremonial outing round the town. The skill with which she countered his half-hearted defence of men he vaguely regarded as colleagues matched her agility over the rocks.

But there was a more interesting chapel on an island in the next cove, she told him. It dated from before the Great Schism, and stones from a pagan temple were incorporated in its walls.

'We could go there,' she said.

Beresford-Evans admired her familiarity with schisms and iconoclasts and basilican plans and he had no doubt that the chapel would be interesting if she said so, but he wasn't going to start trailing about a foreign country with a young girl at his age. He really couldn't impose, he assured her, and he really must write some letters, but he had enjoyed his lunch enormously. And in fact, he realized, after he had left and rejoined the tourists' parade along the front, so he had.

Indeed, he ought to send a few cards. He stopped at the papershop and selected a peasant on a mule for Dodge the churchwarden. Mrs Stiggles who saw to the altar cloths would like an 'art' composition of gay shutters on whitewashed walls – damn the expense – and be pleased to think he was having a lovely rest. Catching sight of the phallic Pan he twitched a smile at the thought of sending it to the Dean, but instead chose the chapel on the clifftop. Back in his room the writing of the cards took a long time, because his mind kept drifting off to review the progressive revelation of an athletic mind that so closely matched a slim but muscular body.

That was how it began. And a week later Beresford-Evans was contemplating the bare feet that lay, soles uppermost, on the dazzling white surfboard in front of him like two neat pink fish on a slab. Semele's feet were among the prettiest things he had seen – and twenty years in a South coast parish where sandals were much worn had taught him that the daintiest of women seldom have pretty feet. His wife's had been chubby and sweet, but these were a delight. And the young Sylvia would have found it deliciously absurd that he, a priest in mourning, should be hanging on the tail end of a surfboard and propelling it over a transparent sea under the direction of the near-naked owner of those feet, who lay prone beyond them – he could almost hear the explosive giggle.

'Nearly there,' came the so-similar voice from the front end of the surfboard. 'Turn in after the big rock.'

Beresford-Evans gave a couple more vigorous kicks, then the board twisted from his hands as Semele rolled off in a flurry of limbs and water. His own feet found bottom and he followed her as she carried the surfboard up the beach, her spine curved and hip jutting in stunning thrust and counterthrust.

They put the basket down in the shade and looked back at the segment of sea flecked with distant sails. They were in a cove on the opposite side of the island from the land. The little chapel was above them.

'Why don't more people come here?' asked Beresford-Evans.

'The local people don't like to – the chapel is not consecrated any more – and the visitors don't know about the cove. It's quite hard to find, even from a boat.'

Beresford-Evans did not think the chapel at all sinister. The whitewashed inside was sunlit, with leaves thrusting in through glassless windows. There was a little domed apse with faint traces of painted figures. All the icons had been taken away, but a jamjar of oil had been left behind and on the iconostasis someone had scratched a little figure with goat's feet.

'Here's your friend again,' said Beresford-Evans.

'You find him everywhere,' replied Semele.

He was irritated at her complacency. 'He's not to be taken seriously, you know. Just a little phallic goatherd terrifying people who interrupt his afternoon nap.'

'Have you never felt it – the fear at midday?'

Beresford-Evans surprised himself with the loudness of his scornful laugh as he followed her down the path. Semele almost swaggered over to where they had spread the towels, stripped off her brassière and stretched herself to offer twin brown sleeknesses to the sun. Beresford-Evans addressed the translucent amber nipples:

'You have to admit it's pretty silly stuff.'

The boyish body gathered its knees and thrust its

heels into the sand.

'It's no sillier than Christianity.'

'Oh, come!' chid Beresford-Evans.

'Well is it? God creates men who are free to do good or evil –'

'That's what's so wonderful!' cried Beresford-Evans.

' – then, when men are bad, God doesn't make them good, which he could easily do. Instead he tortures them eternally – not to reform them, but just for some sort of revenge. Just think of it – torture for ever and ever in return for seventy years' badness! Isn't it a bit – ' she groped for a word – 'a bit "stiff"?'

Beresford-Evans had often thought so: 'Of course, but Christ – '

'Yes, I know – then God reforms and decides to let men off if they're sorry. But instead of telling them about it by sending down another tablet, or something, he interferes with a decent girl –'

'Look, I say –'

' – to get a son who has to be tortured to death to persuade God to do what he has already decided to do. Then – '

Beresford-Evans lay on his back with his eyes closed and wrestled with the absurd arguments that were thrust and levered by a mind that he could not dissociate from the image of the body beside him – a body that he knew, from a convulsion in the sand and a whisper of cotton, was now as naked as that of an ancient gymnast. He looked at her, and found it odd that this sleekness, that would have been only slightly ambiguous in the boy David, should remind him so vividly of Sylvia's sturdy generosity in the black Venetian bed.

Semele had just finished her defence of Judas, who had been exploited as a means to an end and then awarded an exemplary punishment. Now she was off on a new tack, giggling at the idea of God rushing from one lovers' assignation to another, issuing souls duly stamped with original sin at the moment of conception.

'We Anglicans don't think like that,' muttered Beresford-Evans.

'Oh, you Anglicans and Romans and Lutherans and

Orthodox – you start from your absurd premises and look where they lead – the religion of brotherly love ends up killing and torturing more people than the pagans ever did.'

Her mind was a muscular organ, like her legs and spine. It had the sinewy quickness of adolescence, but all Beresford-Evans's experience with truculent teenagers – he had prided himself on the way he took their callow arguments seriously and won their respect – counted for nothing.

She had returned to the cruelty of putting men on earth for so little time, only to condemn them to eternal pain: ' – and don't tell me it's just, this virtue and vice business; not everyone has the same chance. Some people are starving and reared in brutality, some are born deformed and some are crippled by disease –'

'They make their witness,' said Beresford-Evans. (But hadn't Sylvia been bitter just before the end?)

'And if it's too much for them?'

She had raised herself on one elbow to look straight at him, and now she received his assault smiling. She did not seem at all surprised, and her response rendered it a willing encounter between equals. She made love beautifully, and afterwards Beresford-Evans's dismay at his moral lapse was mingled with satisfaction at his physical performance – for it had been a long time.

He was thankful that he had always been reluctant to condemn the unsanctified lovers in his congregation, but still: 'I want to marry you,' he said.

'No you don't,' she replied. 'But you can oil my back.'

Later she let him oil her front as well, and as he put the stopper back in the bottle, he asked 'What's that?'

Semele reached down and touched the little silver line that disappeared into her crisp fleece. Addressing the sky she said: 'That? Oh, that was from my change.'

'Your what?'

'My change – my operation. Until I was about twelve I was – well, like a boy.'

'You were what?'

'I was sort of a boy, but I had this operation.'

'No, seriously . . .' He was not altogether amused.

24

'It's true. I'd always known I was really meant to be a girl, and I kept on about it so my mother finally saw to it – I was about thirteen, actually. She'd had a lot of trouble and didn't like men much.'

'Your mother – you mean you aren't really – '

'Oh, yes I am – well, you should know!' Then she added: 'But I wasn't always.'

'I don't believe it,' said Beresford-Evans.

'Suit yourself,' said Semele, drawing on her pants.

Beresford-Evans watched her bind her breasts with the slightness of her bikini top. 'Why didn't you – '

'Tell you? I suppose you think I should have worn a label!' She picked up the surfboard and carried it to the water's edge, where she balanced the basket on it. 'Are you coming?' she called, and she lay down on the board and shoved off.

Beresford-Evans followed in a daze. 'I don't believe it,' he said again, as he entered the water. He began to swim beside the surfboard, which Semele propelled with long, sweeping strokes of her arms. The smooth board slid easily over the surface, and he was soon left far behind.

When he reached the town beach Beresford-Evans could see no sign of Semele. He supposed she had gone to change, for they had fallen into the habit of parting after their outings and meeting again at the café where they had first sat together. He changed at his hotel, then wandered along the front looking for her. On the beach there were the usual parties of local boys, but despite his classical education he could only see their hard brown bodies as more loutish than ever. On the other hand, the matrons who usually seemed so encumbered with their own flesh struck him as monumentally and magnificently fecund.

'Nothing has changed,' he assured himself; she was still as she had always been, so far as he was concerned. But he knew he did not believe that. She was either a liar or a walking lie. And she did not come to their café at the usual time. Once he thought he heard her laughing, but when he got up to look he saw only a couple disappearing down a sidestreet. He sat over another drink and watched the people returning from the beach, walking dreamily under their burdens of baskets and bundles and rolled umbrellas, dazed by the hours in the sun.

25

He looked across the beach towards the sea, from which the last bathers were withdrawing. Girls emerged from the water and walked towards their lovers, carrying their loins carefully, like chalices. The young men greeted them with casual assurance. Their cups were brimming over, but Beresford-Evans's was irredeemably empty. He would go back to his parish, of course, to minister with the deeper understanding born of a chastening experience. But he could not leave till he had 'had it out with her'. Yes . . . but the turbulent debates that formed in his imagination were more carnal than intellectual.

Disgusted with himself, he got up; and then he saw her. She was lying under the sea wall beside a youth whom he vaguely recognized. Beresford-Evans watched the heads bowing together, then rocking apart – and the sound of her laughter reached him again. He could not know that Semele had just told the story of her glorious fib about the scar on her tummy, but he did know they were laughing at him.

He went back to his room but could not be still, and wandered out in the gathering dusk for another drink. In spite of himself he returned to the promenade, where only a pair of lovers now walked, leaning together and looking gravely out from their private world. From further along came the sound of a flute, and he walked towards it. Two people sitting together under a lamp made a single shape on the sea wall. As he approached, one figure detached itself and moved down the steps that led to the beach; the other continued to play, and when Beresford-Evans drew nearly level he saw it was the youth – a young man, really – who had been with Semele. The young man paused in his playing and grinned at Beresford-Evans, who again had the feeling that he knew that sideways look. Then the lips were pouted to the instrument again and the young man got up, still playing, and went with tripping steps down the stairs towards the sea.

At the top of the steps Beresford-Evans peered down at the beach. It was very dark, but he could make out the line of the sea, and in the sweeping flash of the lighthouse he caught a movement on the sand. When he heard her laughing he climbed heavily down, and in the next flash he saw them – at first he thought it was a monster of some sort, then he realized she was riding on the young man's shoulders. The light passed on, but he heard her laugh again as he moved forward again. The next sweep of light showed them in silhouette, a great double creature – a sort of two-legged centaur – running through the shallows with her hair trailing behind and the man's head, thrust forward under his burden, projecting like a phallus in front.

The sea slapped about his ankles. He pulled off his clothes clumsily as he entered the water. 'Pan is dead!' he told the wave into which he launched himself, 'Great Pan is dead!'

'Great Pan is dead!' he shouted back at the sound of the flute that came across the water. Then he began to repeat it in a steady, gasping chant, in time with his strokes: 'Great Pan – is dead! Great Pan – is dead!' To a peal of laughter that was confused with the sound of the sea he shouted 'Great Pan is dead!'

After a while he became aware of someone swimming beside him.

'Great Pan is dead,' he breathed. 'Great Pan is dead!'

'Of course he is,' replied his wife, and her sturdy limbs wrapped round him under the water.

Ziggy's Last Dance

A red stripe the colour of parrot's blood swam down each side of the face reflected in the pool. He rubbed white clay into the rubbery flatness of nose and, with the charcoal from his pouch, drew black strokes across the deep grooves the years had chiselled in his cheeks. Then he squatted back and pulled a long face as he inserted the fibula into his nose-slit, and finally he grimaced two or three times to settle everything into place. The mist was already rising to the tops of the trees where it suddenly coiled and vanished. It was time to be getting along, for he could not move as fast as he used to. Ziggy stood up, threw his cloak over his shoulder, gathered his things and set off, conscious of his heavy responsibilities.

Halfway round the world, the Commissar in charge of the world's greatest army flushed the lavatory and headed for bed. It was three in the morning, and already everything was demonstrated in a cool, granular light. He was too old for late-night drinking with the Boss, but he had felt obliged – a matter of not giving a damn for the morrow, like the characters in the old stories that began 'In the town of X lived a young officer . . .' He looked in on the girls, sleeping in their one bed like apples stored to ripen, and went to lie down beside Masha. She threw a heavy thigh over him, but he gently turned away. In two hours he would be back at the Command Centre, and it would be like those days at Smolny, but with much more at stake.

Right round the world the face on the pillow resumed its

heaviness. While it was rapt and tossing from side to side the flesh had been drawn taut and the cheekbones thrown into their old prominence, which the Secretary in charge of the world's mightiest military machine found reassuring, for cancellation of his wife's age implied a recovery of his own youth. He disengaged his body from hers and stretched beside her. She murmured polite contentment and turned away. It was still light outside; they had not made love at such an odd hour for years, but he had felt obliged. It was sort of symbolic, when in a little while he would be sitting in the Big Bunker playing the biggest poker game of all.

The leaders of the Hornbill tribe were conferring. The situation was very grave. Ziggy was extremely dangerous; a most competent wizard – more powerful than any other now living; as powerful, perhaps, as the great men of old, who had been kept in check by the constraining net of each other's powers. But now, with the tribe so reduced, and with the Bluejays riddled with disease and the Cockatoos ruined by easy living beside the construction camps, there was no check on Ziggy's power, and he was very angry.

He had left his house. He had taken his magic rods and his pouch and cloak with him. His daughter had said so, glaring at them from her one eye, the other staring whitely. She held out no hope. Ziggy would settle things once and for all, for he was very powerful. More powerful than the Bongas; more powerful than the He and She. If Boolabil had not run off with the girl it would have been different; Ziggy might have been pacified. He might even have seen to the rain. But the girl had desecrated his things and taken his favourite stone. It was not a matter to be settled by talking – in fact it might never be settled.

The villagers had offered to find Boolabil, to beat him very hard and fetch the girl back, but the old woman scorned the idea. Ziggy could not be pacified as easily as that. It was a matter of principle – he himself was bound by it.

That was this morning. Since then they had hunted down Boolabil and the girl, smeared them with filth and paraded them round the village, shouting dreadful insults. They called the girl a dried fig and Boolabil an utterer of his father's name. Then they marked them as outcasts and chased them away with sticks. No one would receive them; they would die miserably. Ziggy would know, but it would make no difference.

There was no doubt that Ziggy had gone to the rocks where the He and the She dwelt. He would have clambered into the midst of the chaos, up to the solitary tree. If he were strong enough to go through with it – to take all the necessary steps – it would be the end of everything. The Bongas would be powerless to prevent it and there was no wizard but Ziggy nowadays. If his nephew had not gone to ride the big yellow machine for the white men things might have been different. The young man had been a promising wizard, but now his powers had been dried up by the yellow sun beyond the forest; they had been driven away by the insane roaring of the yellow machine.

It was strange that such a wizard as Ziggy should have arisen now, just when the tribes were dying. But of course, it was meant to be. Thus the white men, who had dispossessed the Bongas and sealed the fate of the people had, by removing all the constraints on Ziggy, sealed their own fate as well.

A young man suggested that a party should set out for the rocks to kill Ziggy before he could carry out his intentions. For such impiety the youth was beaten and forbidden to speak again.

But perhaps if they were to steal the proscribed maiden of the Bluejays . . . ? She was reputed to have breasts like melons and hips like a forest buffalo. She could be washed and oiled and properly decked out and offered to Ziggy. He might accept and relent. Even if he didn't, he might be mollified a little. Of course, it would mean trouble with the Bluejays and, although they were a sickly lot, some of them had guns. Wars that actually involved killing people were an affront to the Bongas as well as bad manners, but even a war to the death would be worthwhile if it stopped Ziggy.

Someone suggested that when they had stolen the girl they should sacrifice her to the He and She. She was, after all, very valuable. It seemed a pity, but if they did it properly, the more she cried the more likely were the Powers to be persuaded. But

Warramunga the Headman said that the speaker did not understand things at all. In such an affair as this not only the Bongas, but even the He and the She were powerless. Ziggy was working on the very Nature of Things. They should attack the Bluejays before daybreak tomorrow. They only wanted the girl, but if necessary they would kill all the men and hang the women and children on the thorns like lizards set to dry. There was time for the Wamba dance and the Washing of the Spears before they set off.

Then came the news that Ziggy had enchanted the brother of Boolabil and carried him away. The two of them had been seen by the women from the fields, moving in the direction of the painted rocks. The women had known Ziggy by his wizard's cloak and his lopsided old-man's gait, and the young man was stumbling behind him, evidently entranced. The elders shook their heads. That meant Ziggy intended to do it properly. Arunta said Ziggy would turn the brother of Boolabil into a great bird with its blood on the outside of its body in place of feathers, and the bird would fly down and peck away the foundations of the World. Warramunga had a vague idea that the boy's body would be turned into a roaring emptiness into which everything would rush like water into a whirlpool. Neither of them really knew anything, except that at the heart of the work would be a long, long, intricate dance that only a wizard like Ziggy could perform. It would be a great undertaking, but Ziggy was extraordinary, and probably capable of it despite his age.

The leaders of the Socialist and truly Democratic World – the real Free World – conferred in words that had the slushy, shuffling sound of boots in wet snow. The broad, catlike faces sipped tea and blinked through the smoke of brown-paper cigarettes. They acknowledged the importance of anticipation and the need to keep the challenge nicely attuned to the risk. They must maintain diplomatic contact even while demonstrating resolve. A young man of about fifty who suggested they should make more use of the official international organizations was scornfully silenced.

The sad, pale men in sad, dark suits weighed the advantages of rapid deployment of numerical superiority against the risk of a tactical nuclear counterstroke. They explored the possibility of a pre-emptive strategic strike – 'not an ideal scenario, gentlemen, but after all, to possess weapons is to intend to use them . . . '

The metropolitans fidgeted while the statutory provincials affirmed their support for Central Policy and Revolutionary Orthodoxy. A dashing moustache's bravura on how the Nature of Things was on their side brought a sharp reminder that they were concerned with military facts. The moustache insisted that military facts flowed from the Nature of Things and proposed the immediate Liquidation of the Aggressor through a Pre-emptive Counterforce and Counter-city Strike of Massive Proportions.

The old man at the head of the table put down his glass of tea, buttoned his upper lip over his lower, then unbuttoned it again to sibilate that no one questioned the inevitability of Victory to the Great Patriotic Struggle –

'And to Socialism!' interjected the moustache.

– And to Socialism, which was of course the same thing. But for the moment they were concerned with crude and immediate material considerations. They were, after all, materialists by profession and conviction. It fell to them to conduct a ruthless diplomatic and military campaign on behalf of all the peoples of the world, including the so-called non-aligned peoples and including even the so-called enemy peoples – and of course including those helpless peoples who had not yet reached the level of political consciousness. Their National Destiny was to lead the international masses forward to Victory, no matter what the cost. The Soul of the Nation called out for it!

Everyone present thought of the Soul of the Nation and the Fearless Patriotic Struggle; of smoked fish and pasties, of deep-breasted women with haunches like mares, of damp, affectionate children and the demands of ruthless, egg-smashing, omelette-making strategy. Maps were rolled down from the ceiling and rolled up again to be replaced by others. Markers were pushed about on tables like chips in a casino. The atmosphere was one of elated gravity.

The leaders of the true Free World – the really Democratic World – were conferring. These were not the polyglot bunch of allies who pretended to be the source and the custodians of Western Culture; these were the real men of power. They wore their hair cropped short, because they were practical men. The plump cheeks of the younger ones derived, not from an excess of steak and icecream, but from a healthy childhood of gumchewing. More than half of those present were not young at all, and had faces as fissured and eroded as ancient deserts. Some wore brightly coloured lounge suits, and the rest wore drab lounge-uniforms. Apart from the urgent twanging of the metropolitans, they all spoke in a flat, deliberate plod like the march of the Foreign Legion.

A man with the craggy face of pilgrim stock and a banking fortune was in the middle of an intricate analysis. Suddenly he stopped short and broke out in a boyish grin.

'Hell!' he said. 'I say we nuke'em righdaway!'

Cries of assent and dissent gave way before the rising utterance of a face as fissured as the mud-caked groin of a prairie buffalo. The face punched out, in single-word slugs, that it did not think, as of that time, that they could afford to mess with chicken-shit reactions, and it agreed with Mr Winthrop here that, as of now –

'But we godda tahk toom fuchrissake!' cried a diplomat.

'Ain't no use tahk'n toom,' said the ancient face, 'We godda show we got balls!'

But they did talk, at least to each other, of tripwires and thresholds and credibility, of 'bahms' on hard and soft targets, of projected casualties, of five-for-one city threats and the problem of finding enough cities, of denying facilities to the enemy by the pre-emptive destruction of allied territory – Hell! If you wanted to defend values you had to expect it to cost!

They, too, rolled maps down from the ceiling and pushed markers about on tables. They, too, sipped and smoked, though some cosseted their health by taking no sugar in their coffee and abstaining from cigarettes. They reflected that Gahd would ensure their ultimate victory, and they took inspiration from their role as defenders of Freedom and Democracy and Our Way of Life. They thought of real, deep, home-baked pies, of young women with gumchewers' cheeks and bodies like marzipan, whose nudity when unwrapped was emphasized by the pale shadows of bikinis. They thought with chaste affection of sexually precocious little girls, until the companion-thought of combatively precocious little boys brought them back to calculations of megadeaths.

Ziggy looked at the man who hung in the thorn tree. At last he was quiet. The paint Ziggy had daubed him with was beaded with sweat and blood, and the draggled feathers stirred slightly as the night air passed over them. It would not be long now. He had cried dreadfully at first – that was necessary, of course, for it was a distressingly painful ceremony and the man had been very strong, so it had taken a long time. Even Ziggy, who took a professional view of these things, had felt pity for him. But it had to be.

Now Ziggy was very tired. He had taken all the necessary steps, but it was really too much for one old man. In days gone by there would have been a team of wizards, but then, of course, there would have been rival teams working against them all the time. Well he, Ziggy, had not been hindered, for he was the last wizard. His worst moment had been when he discovered that the egg – very necessary – that he had brought in his pouch was broken. But a juri bird had led him to her nest – though it involved a climb and he had slipped and twisted his ankle. Then the dance. It was a very intricate, long dance – far too much for one man, especially an old man with a twisted ankle. But he, Ziggy, had managed it, though it had lasted nearly till dawn.

And now it was all done – just a matter of waiting. It seemed a pity in many ways. It was the Hornbills' fault, but the punishment was too severe and too general. There really should have been other wizards to protect the people. That there were none was because of the white men, but they could not really be blamed. They had their white Bongas, of which Ziggy under-stood nothing. In a way he felt more sorry for them than any-one else, for they would never understand what was happening to them.

Ziggy touched a circle of grey rag that hung round his neck. He had got it from a young white woman who had come with some others – the only white people Ziggy had actually seen – chasing insects and peering at birds and trying to catch their Bongas in black boxes. What was now a ragged cloth necklace had then covered the whole of the top half of Ziggy's body, and had borne the magic sign ⊕. But that was many years ago and, like the forest, the garment had gradually dwindled away. He had only given a woven bark box for it – the girl was an evident fool – but it was very precious to him.

The hanging man shuddered. It was not quite over, but it was very close now.

The Commissar for Defence was proud of the fact that he could walk in the square under the clustered towers and not be stared at, let alone be interviewed, jostled, molested or pelted with eggs – though that, of course, would have struck any sane person as an absurd waste of eggs. Naturally, he would not cross the square alone, even at this early hour. He had Vassily with him and a few paces behind and out of earshot, a couple of guards.

The long session had closed after the decision to start the final diplomatic sequence – the sequence that would lead, if there were no accommodation, straight into Operation Sasha. Of course, it was now forbidden for anyone to leave the bunker, but he enforced the rules, so he was exempt. Besides, if anyone from the Higher Apparatus saw him in the square it would be good for morale, and if the other side spotted him from one of their satellites, so much the better. The Commissar chuckled at the idea. He wondered if he dared snatch a few minutes with Masha and the girls, decided it would be unwise, and tried to think of parallels to his position from history, or from the great novels.

Across the North Pole another meeting was breaking up. Since a Red Alert could not be maintained indefinitely, a sequence of diplomatic steps had been planned. No deadline would be announced, but it was decided that if no satisfactory reaction was received within three hours of the last step in the sequence, Operation Mary Lou would automatically be inaugurated. As of now, no one would leave the complex, and all unofficial lines to the outside were closed.

The men moved towards the door in twos and threes, with more pauses for jollier talk and louder laughter than usual. They quietened down in the lift to the amenity floor, but once there they set about ordering drinks with irrepressible bonhomie.

The Secretary for Defence took his fruit juice and strolled out to the panoramic window on the other side of a concrete screen. The chief Hawk joined him, and they looked out at the city together.

'You get a great sunset up here,' said the chief Hawk.

They stood at the window as the rim of sun slid down, and watched for the moment of its disappearance.

'All those colours,' said the Secretary. 'They're just because of the . . . ' He said 's-m-o-g' in a low tone, and very slowly, as the sun, which he had just seen disappear, rose again and continued to rise at an accelerating pace, expanding in a geometric progression as it did so.

'The bastards!' breathed the chief Hawk. Then he yelled at the top of his voice, shaking his fists above his head at the sheer injustice:

'The bastards pre-empted us!'

The shadow of his spreadeagled rage was printed on the concrete wall behind him, and was to stay there, under the moss that covered it in a few years, for a score of centuries, until it was erased by the slow erosion of the surface.

The onion domes gleamed in the early morning sun. How they gleamed! The men walking in the square stopped and watched as the gold turned red, then brilliant white, and seemed to run before their eyes. For a moment the Commissar thought of Masha's breasts that had fed the girls, and he saw, not molten

37

gold, but their fat melting and burning. He breathed an obscenity as if it were a holy name:

'The — idiots! Don't they know the rules?'

Then there was no answer, and no Commissar to look for one.

Warramunga the Headman had sensed it coming. The air had changed. The forest had shivered as the Bongas, knowing it was the end, moved in the trees. For five seconds, before the searing light from the wrong end of the sky snapped his body back like a grasshopper caught in a bush-fire, he bent forward in admiring laughter. Ziggy had done it! He was indeed a great wizard.

At Manoli's Sheepfold

The sun beat on the landscape as if to flatten it. The mountains stood firm, though shadows were obliterated and colours washed away by the intensity of light. It was a long way to the refuge, and their packs were heavy with a full store of food, including tomatoes and peaches and an emergency supply of sweets and raisins that Julie was sure they would never get through. There was a spare cylinder of gaz, too, in Nancy's pack, because she said they couldn't be sure of finding the right size in remote places. She cheered Julie on by pointing out that their loads could only get lighter as they ate their way through them.

It was the hottest part of the day, but at least there were springs by the path, each announced in advance by the musical running of water into a sheep-trough. At the last village they had drunk coffee; a cheerful old man had invited them into a backyard under a vine, to be served by a cheerful old wife. Since then they had seen no one except a woman who had overtaken them on a horse, her sturdy russet legs rocking stiffly as she sat sideways in the wooden pack-saddle. She had a surprisingly youthful face, when she raised it to shout a greeting to where they rested in the shade of a clump of alders. They could still see her, in the distance and on foot now, loping up eagerly through the stunted trees of the hillside opposite. She was urging the horse in front of her towards a low cabin in the midst of a sheep-trodden clearing, where a man stood waiting.

The refuge they were making for came into sight, sparkling white on the shoulder of the mountain, but there was still a tantalizingly protracted zigzag approach and an offensively steep last stretch before they could ease their rucksacks down on to the terrace and Nancy could test the frail key in the rusty lock of the sheet-iron door. After an anxious moment, it turned.

Inside, it was quite cool, perhaps because the refuge had lain in the shadow of the mountain all morning. Now they opened the iron shutters and warm sunlight flooded across the long table and benches. There was a dormitory, redolent of Baden-Powell austerities, a kitchen with some battered pots and pans, a meagre stock of wood down in the cellar and, alongside that, two grimly purposeful latrines.

On the terrace that looked out on the sheer face of the mountain they luxuriated like cats in the sun. They ate, commending with the white *fetta* cheese for the fresh astringency that went so well with olives, and enjoying the breeze that was gently funnelling over the col. The refuge was on the very crest, and the ground fell away in precipices on either side, except for the path by which they had come and another that led down to the high plateau that lay beyond the ridge.

'That's called *Stani tou Manoli*,' said Nancy, poring over the guidebook, 'which apparently means "Manoli's sheepfold". There's supposed to be a lake over there somewhere . . . there is is, look. That's the end of it, sticking out from behind that hillock.' She read some more, and added 'It's very deep and there's a dragon at the bottom.'

Marvellously recovered, after the food – though Julie thought it might have been the tonic air – they tried their legs and discovered an almost levitated ease of movement without their packs.

'Who's for a walk to the lake, then?' said Nancy.

They reached it quite quickly. It was surprisingly big, but cunningly hidden by folds in the ground; very blue, and lapping at its margins with decorously liquid sounds. They mooned about, dabbling in the shallows, then offered their pale northern limbs on two smooth stone altars – Nancy, who had foreseen the possibility, in her bikini and Julie in shorts and bra. Presently Nancy sat up.

'I'm going in,' she said.

'It'll be cold,' said Julie, opening her eyes and looking at the water. Colours were always washed out when the sun had been beating through your eyelids, but the blue seemed exceptionally pale over on the far side. Could there be a bed of ice under the water? 'And it might not be as clean as it looks,' she added. 'There's sheep about.'

'It can't be any dirtier than I am,' said Nancy, and hissed at the chill as she waded in. Then, with a flurry and a yell she was swimming. From Julie's hot rock it looked delicious.

'Come on!' shouted Nancy.

Julie took off her shorts then, after a moment's hesitation and a quick glance at a sheep, who immediately stopped staring and returned to cropping the thin grass, the rest of her clothes – there was no point in getting them wet. The pebbly mud at the edge of the lake was not unpleasant to walk on, but the water was cold on her ankles and the shock as she waded deeper made her gasp.

'It's freezing!' she shouted at the back of Nancy's bobbing head, then thought it would make a good picture and went back to fetch her camera. Nancy whooped and splashed, rolling over in the water. Conscious of the din they were making in this wilderness Julie looked round. She stiffened in horror, threw the camera ashore and plunged into the water. Nancy turned and saw Julie's cleft bottom, pink as a peach with the chill, approaching across the agitated surface; then her sleeked head emerged.

'There's people!' she said.

There were indeed. A dark figure, cowled like a monk, was leaning on a staff and looking at them from a couple of hundred yards away. He was joined by another, emerging from behind the hillock.

'What'll we do?' asked Julie, shivering.

'I'm getting out,' said Nancy. 'It's them that's intruding.' She swam to the edge and clambered out and back on her rock to dry in the sun.

'It's all right for you!' wailed Julie.

'Oh, to Hell!' Nancy slithered to the ground and turned her back to the figures who still stared fixedly, each leaning on his staff. Not bothering to make of the rock more than a token concealment, she whipped off her bikini and dried herself perfunctorily with her shirt before pulling it on. Meanwhile Julie, emboldened by the demonstration, emerged from the water, scurried across to her clothes and slithered into them, leaving most of her drying till she felt the reassurance of cloth on her skin.

A shrill voice came from the direction of the watchers, and the girls turned to see them skulking away, scolded by the bobbing head of a woman, who presently emerged in her entirety – and the horse beneath her – from behind the hillock. It was the same woman that had overtaken them earlier, but now she looked at them stonily as she passed and rapped out 'Kalispera' like an accusation in response to their greeting.

'She thinks we're scarlet women come to ensnare her men,' said Julie with relish.

'She couldn't be more wrong,' said Nancy. The men had stopped to stare again; she smiled falsely and waved, polishing the air at them. There was no response, except that one man fluttered the fingers of one hand, still held down by his side. They didn't seem very attractive prey.

The girls giggled once or twice as they started back, then forgot the encounter as they dodged about, finding vantage points from which to photograph the mountain, the lake, the panorama of peaks that closed the horizon, and each other. They realized now that the landscape was peopled with at least three flocks and perhaps four shepherds, stalking like bishops in their great hooded cloaks and each presiding over a woolly congregation to whom he presumably counted as God. None of the men responded to waves or shouted greetings, but stood gravely staring, leaning on staffs that the girls now perceived were crooks.

At the refuge Nancy chopped logs in the cellar with a broken axe and got a fire going in the stove, while Julie stewed desiccated vegetables into edibility. They ate and became sleepy, but when they went out on the terrace for a last look at the landscape they found the shepherds still there in the distance. One was a monklike silhouette on the skyline; another was bringing some sheep along the stream that ran through the plateau below – his shouts to his dogs rose thinly – and a third was moving through the jumbled rocks higher up. When Julie, having looked away, looked back for him, she found he had covered a surprising amount of ground, yet he moved over the broken surface without apparent haste, his boots slowly pacing below the skirt of the great cloak.

In the middle of the night they both woke. Something had clattered, and there was a scuffling from the terrace outside.

'Did you bolt the door?' hissed Julie.

'You were the last out.'

Reluctantly Julie began to wriggle out of her sleeping-bag, but Nancy was already padding off, swearing as she stubbed a toe on a stray boot. She came back muttering that all was in order and the door firmly fastened.

'Do you suppose they stay up all night?' asked Julie.

'Who?'

'The shepherds. Do they stay with their sheep all the time, do you think?'

'Perhaps.'

Julie drifted back into sleep, thinking of the shepherds circling like stars on one of those old-fashioned models of the solar-system – an orrery, was it? It was disturbing, but not altogether disagreeable to think there were human beings out there, cowled like storybook wizards and mediating between oneself indoors and the Wild Forces of Nature outside.

'We did have a visitor,' said Nancy next morning, when she returned from her first scurrying expedition out of doors. She was holding up a grubby-looking paper bag. 'This was on the doorstep.'

'What is it?'

'Eggs. Funny ones.'

They were very small; sharply pointed at one end and dark, with even darker blotches.

'What are they?' asked Nancy. Julie knew all about flowers, so it seemed reasonable to ask her about eggs. But Julie had no idea, except that they were rather beautiful. Nancy liked things definite, so 'They're plovers' eggs,' she said. They fried half a dozen for breakfast and found them delicious. But they put off going down to the plateau to thank their benefactors till after they had climbed the mountain.

To do that they had to retrace a little of their path of yesterday, then circle up to take the peak from behind. On the track below the refuge they met two mules, one ridden by a thin man whose legs dangled below the sacks and boxes slung across the animal's shoulders, the other bearing a fat man who sat far back, a gross insult to its slim, labouring haunches.

'*Yassas*,' called the girls, feeling warm towards these companions of the egg-bringers.

'*Yah!*'

The reply was curt and unsmiling, and the mules laboured on unchecked. Julie developed a theory that isolation made people shy and prone to conceal goodwill in gruffness.

The mountain was easy. Behind the first outcrop was another, higher plateau that carried them up until, after a final scramble, they were at the top of the tremendous cliff-face that overhung the refuge. They could see it far below; a tiny cube surrounded by barren slopes dotted with rocks and – yes, those were minuscule sheep with a tiny black figure in attendance. Then everything was swept away as a cloud blundered over the peak.

On the way back a couple of shepherds loomed at a distance through the mist, sheep drifting round their skirts and huge dogs bristling and barking in front. Then the girls emerged into bright sunlight again. They tried a different way down, past a small lake in a fold of the mountainside, and lost their way.

'There's a hut,' said Julie, and they hurried towards this human outpost. Two men in the doorway watched their approach, and a young boy came out and shouted at the dog that stood, stiff-maned and snarling.

'*Kalimera*,' said Nancy.

'*Kalimera*,' said the boy.

'*Yah*,' said the men.

The girls launched into their phrasebook rigmarole for asking the way and were answered by jabbing arms and nods that evidently meant they were to carry straight on. The two groups faced each other. The girls groped for words, but were distracted by an awareness that the air was burdened by a sharp stench and the buzzing of innumerable blue flies. Then one of the men asked a question and the boy was ordered to translate:

'How long are you in Greece?'

'Three weeks – we've been here one week and we have two weeks more.'

The boy was confused, but reported something or other back. Another question rapped out immediately, and yes, the girls replied, they had come by *aeroplano* . . .

No, it carried fifty. . . How long? Oh, about two hours . . . The fare was –

'Ten thousand drachmas.' Nancy decided that was near enough.

'How much money did you bring with you to Greece?'

They hesitated. 'We – we brought travellers' cheques,' said Julie.

'Travellers' cheques. Hm, hm,' said the men.

'*Yasas*,' said Nancy, and turned to go.

'*Yah!*' said the men.

The boy ran ahead to show the way, and as he passed her Julie caught that smell again and dropped back a pace. Presently the boy stopped and pointed down to where two mules, each with a man on its rump and what appeared to be a coffin slung on each side, were climbing towards them. Taken by surprise, Julie came too close to the boy, inhaled a lungful of his atmosphere, and retched.

'Whatever is it?' she gasped to Nancy.

'Sheep, I suppose,' but Nancy spoke without conviction.

The boy had hurried on, but now he rushed forward to embrace the older muleteer – his grandfather, probably – who enfolded him in his arms. Julie retched again at the sight.

'How can they?'

'They probably don't notice,' said Nancy.

And as they passed the little caravan all was explained. The coffins were the source of a fierce and eloquent animal pungency; they could only be cheeseboxes. No doubt they were on their way to the hut to be filled with the *fetta* that was made there, and that would garnish a thousand delicate salads on the coast in a few days' time.

The boy turned back with the muleteers, and a little later the girls, who had been looking forward to lunching on cheese a few minutes before, ate dry bread with their olives and hurried on. They were tired by the time they reached the hut, and fit only for bed when they had finished the beautifully moist omelette that Julie made with the rest of the eggs.

'We still haven't thanked them,' she said.

'Tomorrow,' said Nancy. 'Before we set off.' For they were pushing on next day.

They slept undisturbed, and there were no eggs next morning. But when, booted for departure, they had finally dragged their rucksacks outside and locked the iron door, a man suddenly stood up from where he must have been sitting under the parapet of the terrace.

'*Kalimera*,' they said.

'*Kalimera*,' said the man. He was the thin muleteer they had met on the track the day before. Now he gave a low whistle, but instead of a dog his fat companion came, deliberately placing his crook as he padded across the rocks. Before he reached the terrace another shepherd had sprung on to it from the other side. Now two more, one of them the grandfather of the boy at the cheese hut, came up the path out of the hollow below the refuge. And there was the boy, sidling round the corner of the building; Julie instinctively shifted her rucksack to bring it between herself and him.

The girls *Kalimera*'d, nodding and grinning nervously. There was a low murmur of greeting from the men; Julie thought she recognized one of the watchers at the lake, now with a gun under his arm.

'Thank you for the eggs,' said Nancy. '*Efharisto . . . avgi . . .*' But of course, the boy was there and could translate. His doing so brought more murmurs from the men, accompanied by nods and a few shy smiles.

'They say,' said the boy, 'you are worth a few eggs.'

The men growled confirmation and edged forward. The girls smiled foolishly. Julie saw with apprehension what Nancy had already observed: both paths down from the hut were blocked by men leaning on crooks. Everywhere else there were precipices, except at the very foot of the mountain face, and in the last few minutes the jumble of rocks that lay there had been invested with a flock of sheep, attended by a shepherd and two dogs.

'They want you,' said the boy.

The man with the gun smiled, revealing surprisingly good teeth. The fat man grinned and hitched up his belt; Julie noticed that his teeth were well looked after too, at least to the extent that most of them were gold.

'They want to take you,' said the boy, and several more men grinned, squared their shoulders and hitched up their belts.

Nancy found herself thinking that the worst of it was that the people who had said girls shouldn't travel alone in Greece would be proved right. Then she considered that there were six of them not counting the boy and decided that the 'I told you so's' would not be the worst of it.

'You mean,' she said to the boy, 'us – with them?'

'With all of them,' said the boy, and added 'And me.'

Julie was wondering if it would be six-and-a-half each or a share-out. She looked at the grandfather, beak-nosed in his cowl, and remembered the smell at the cheese hut. Would she be able to hold her breath all the time? She doubted it, and knew she would die.

The fat man was beckoning. The boy tugged Julie's sleeve, but Nancy stepped forward in her place.

'Don't upset them,' said Julie.

'All right,' said Nancy, and stood facing the men.

The thin man leaned across to fatty and said something out of the corner of his mouth. The fat man listened, eyeing Nancy's lower body, and other men shuffled their feet and turned away to hide their grins. The fat man jerked his head sideways in the way that signifies assent in Greece, and said something to the boy.

'Trousers!' said the boy, pointing to Nancy's culottes.

'Oh, God!' thought Julie, 'its really happening!'

The thing was, to spin it out as long as possible, Nancy had decided. A climbing party might appear on the path below at any moment. She bent and began slowly to unlace her boots.

'*Ohi, ohi!*' The thin man forbade the removal of boots with a dismissively wagging finger. The fat man stabbed his stubby index at the culottes.

As Nancy instinctively turned away to undo them Julie saw that some of the men, too, looked aside. Then they gradually raised their eyes again to where Nancy, standing in the tight shorts that she usually stripped to in the heat of the day, was folding the culottes with great deliberation. Still she played for time. Perhaps a helicopter would come round the mountain – they had seen a helicopter only the day before yesterday. People were always coming up here; there was no reason why they should not arrive at this moment instead of any other.

Having carefully refolded the discarded culottes two or three times Nancy bent to brush away an imaginary smudge on her thigh, and before she could straighten up the fat man shot out an arm and pulled her to him. Off balance, she found herself held tight against his side, gripped round the waist and half covered with his cloak. She noticed that it was woven with a thick pile inside and out. She also perceived that this man, too, had been involved in cheesemaking, and she breathed as shallowly as possible. She looked across at Julie, who stood ashen.

And for a moment nothing happened. Julie faced the row of men, with the fat one in the middle clutching Nancy, who was grinning bravely at her with clenched teeth. Julie resented the stubborn solidity of the ground under her feet and longed to faint. The men were making urging motions to her now. Grinning at her . . . such a lot of gold teeth!

'Take! Take!' shouted the boy, and tugged at the camera that hung round Julie's neck. Then he ran back to squat in front of the row of men.

'I think they want a picture to record the occasion,' said Nancy, faintly.

Hesitating, Julie raised the camera, then found she had not opened the case. She fumbled, and at last focused on the absurd scene. Snap! It was incredible. Snap! Absurd. Snap!

48

Ridiculous! Her thumb worked furiously, winding on the film. Snap! Snap! There were thirty-six shots in the camera . . . But the men were waving their hands in front of their faces and the boy was tugging at her sleeve shouting '*Endaxi*! Okay!'

Nancy was cast forth and the camera thrust into her hands; Julie was seized in her place. Wonderingly, the girls went through the procedure with their roles reversed; Julie gulping and holding her breath, Nancy making a long pantomime of focusing and taking extra shots from different angles. Then Julie was released and the line of men dissolved. '*Efharisto*!' they cried. '*Endaxi*! Okay!'

'I think . . .' said Julie, uncertainly.

'. . . that they just wanted their pictures taken,' sighed Nancy.

There was a moment of doubt when the fat leader flung off his cloak and unbuttoned the voluminous military jacket he wore underneath. As he fumbled deeper into the layers of clothing the girls wondered if it was all about to start again, but then he fetched out a tattered parcel of newspaper and graciously proffered it. Nancy took it, and found liquid seeping into her hand. She opened one end of the package and peered inside at a moist, crumbling white mass. Her nose flashed its message:

'*Fetta*!' she cried, with hysterical enthusiasm. 'How lovely! *Poli Kalla! Efharisto*!'

The girls joined shrilly and extravagantly in the congratulatory laughter, then the thin man made scribbling motions with his fingers and the fat man levered a flat stone from the top of the terrace wall. He scratched on it with another stone.

'It's his name,' said Julie, peering from a discreet distance.

'*Fotografia*,' said the boy, and handed her the stone.

The girls nodded vigorously to the men. 'Of course – we'll send copies.' They peered at the scratches on the stone and Nancy painfully transliterated as Julie wrote in her diary. 'Konstantinos Manoli,' she spelled out, and an address in the village down the valley. 'Ah, "*Stani tou Manoli*" ' – and she pointed to the plateau below. The men nodded and pointed to themselves. 'Manoli,' they said.

'I do believe they're all one family,' said Nancy. 'They must have been here for generations.'

The company – the Manoli brothers – was already dispersing. On the path below the woman had come into sight, approaching sidesaddle on her laden horse. Julie swung her rucksack on to her back and waved. The woman waved back: her men were safe now.

The girls descended the path on the other side of the ridge, then turned right to cross the plateau and leave by the stony col at the opposite end from the lake. When they reached the crest they looked back. A hooded figure on the skyline by the refuge raised a hand. They waved to him – and to the two others down below, with the flock. The figures waved back. Then the girls went on over the col.

'How soon can we dump this bloody cheese?' asked Nancy.

The Ugliest Man in the World

I first saw him in the underpass by the old Park Hotel. That was years ago, before the redevelopment. He was reluctantly concluding a farewell – body turned to go, but head twisted yearningly back and one arm outstretched to the woman whose hand he was slowly relinquishing. Her arm was extended too, but she was leaning away in a gentle motion of withdrawal. For a moment they reminded me of Michelangelo's 'Creation of Adam' – which was absurd, because they were standing in an underpass, not lolling on clouds; the naked splendour of Adam was replaced by the mundane figure of a plain woman in a cheap coat, and the majestic visage of Jehovah by a bloated, rubber-lipped, broken-nosed mask.

After that I saw them occasionally, always at lunchtime and always in or near the underpass. They did not embrace or make any carnal gestures but came, walking quite quickly, with hands clasped in semi-concealment at the ends of arms held stiffly to their sides. Then they parted, again quite quickly, but with extreme reluctance, gazing into each other's eyes for a moment after their hands had severed, then turning and going off in different directions.

I once met him as he came up the steps from leaving her. He came briskly, with his extravagantly energetic, waddling walk and a trance-like expression suffusing his gross features with melancholy sweetness. It was then that I christened him 'the Ugliest Man in the World'.

After a time they stopped appearing together. In fact, I lost sight of the woman completely, but I continued to see the Ugliest Man, energetically propelling his thick body about the town. His limbs seemed clogged to the point of inefficiency with their own muscle, and he thrashed his way along, one arm held tightly behind him, the other churning the air. His puffy eyes looked fixedly ahead. I didn't know what he did, but supposed he had some clerical post with one of the big mills. Perhaps he had some petty seniority, because his work seemed to involve leaving the office, presumably for business appointments, quite a bit.

I wondered if he had married the woman. That would explain the end of their lunchtime meetings, and perhaps his distant expression as he walked about. He might be contemplating his connubial bliss in a spec-built Dream Home somewhere among the wheeling crescents and avenues of the new suburbs. I imagined him hurrying home to the meals she had lovingly prepared, and sharing their neat hearth with her until she went to prepare the bedtime cocoa. I preferred to pass over the rest with a vague hope that reverence tempered his embraces and that she had the sense to close her eyes on his labouring pig's face.

Then I lost touch with them for a long time. My firm sent me abroad for some years and when I came back our office had been moved to the outskirts of town. Naturally, I had by then forgotten about the Ugliest Man in the World and his courtship or marriage or whatever it was. But one evening, going to an official 'do' at the Assembly rooms with Robbie Penwarden the accountant, I was nearly knocked over by a man who leapt clumsily from a taxi and turned, free arm churning the air, to help someone follow him. Despite the immaculate cut of the dark pinstripe I recognized the thick body and the set of the head on the heavy neck, and slowed down to see who was with him. I suppose I hoped it was the woman from the underpass, though I was apprehensive about seeing her dolled up and aged by several years.

I need not have worried. What emerged from the taxi was a creature dressed with expensive reticence. I caught a glimpse of silken legs educated to grace and dignity, even in descending from a car. Of course, it was not her.

Robbie had noticed my interest. 'Do you know her?' he asked.

'No, who is she?'

'You know him, surely?'

I reminded him that I was out of touch. I thought I knew the man from years ago, but he had hardly cut such a figure in those days.

'He's the next Mayor,' said Robbie.

'Good Lord!' I knew I had lost touch with local affairs, but really . . . 'Who's the lady, then?' – as if I hadn't guessed.

'His wife, of course.'

Just as I feared. A touch of success, and the plain girl jilted.

'She's a stunner, isn't she?' said Robbie, whose slang became dated when he spoke of the, to him, mysterious subject of women.

I admitted that she was not at all bad. 'I can't think what she saw in him, though.'

'Nor me.'

No doubt we both had the same bitter thought about money.

'Anyway,' confided Robbie, 'he seems quite a goer. You should see his secretaries.'

It was sad. The frog had not turned out to be a prince in disguise and Cinderella was not transformed. I put the matter out of my mind in disgust.

But I was not allowed to forget it for long. About a year after my return from abroad the firm became involved in local contracts, and I had to spend a good deal of time in the business circles of the town. Naturally, I often met the new Mayor, and the Mayoress, who really was as charming as she appeared. That made it rather shocking when I first saw the Mayor lunching with another woman – a young girl, in fact. Then I saw him with another, and realized there was nothing in it. He was simply being nice to the girls from the office. In his avuncular manner there was just a touch of the reformed cannibal who might at any moment lapse and sink his teeth into a shoulder. I suppose the girls liked that. Then once, with a sad girl I hadn't seen before, he was solicitous, like a very carnal priest winning a soul. But at no time was there a vestige of that melancholy earnestness that had struck me so at those partings years before.

Still, it did make the monster more intriguing. I asked questions, and learned that he had risen in the world by calculation – literally, for like Robbie he was an accountant. He had studied at evening classes when it was easier to qualify than it is nowadays. That was just about the time that tight financial control became the fashion, and accountants replaced inventors and turned manufacturing into the solving of 'cash-flow problems'.

He had started by 'pulling round' a section of his firm that had 'gone adrift'. On the basis of that he had taken over the general management of what was then a smallish enterprise – but at a time when rivals were in trouble and ready to be bought up. It was an admirable success story, and the marriage had crowned it. The girl was the daughter of a family firm he had taken over and saved from the receivers. He had saved the family bacon and she, by marrying him, had helped him bring in more, for she was a great social asset.

But I became convinced that there was more to the marriage than convenience. As we sat through official functions I used to see them, often separated by chasms of official worthiness, exchanging glances that were almost conspiratorial. When they were together he treated her with something like reverence, and when he was unaware she sometimes looked at him in a way that one associates, not with a wife, but with a young girl contemplating her idol.

An admirable success indeed. Robbie Penwarden suggested that the rapidity of the rise had depended, not only on astuteness and hard work – everyone had to grant him both, as well as luck – but also on a streak of ruthlessness. Of course, Robbie attributed his own lack of progress to an excess of decency and scruple. But even he never suggested that the Ugliest Man's actions were worse than accepted practice.

'But it's the same with the women,' said Robbie.

'How do you mean?'

'It's sheer brass neck. He's so open about everything that people think it must be – well – all right.'

'Perhaps it is.'

'Not all of it.'

Robbie is a confirmed bachelor and not very sound on relations between the sexes. I laughed, but he persisted: 'They say he has another woman in P. . . . You know, a regular establishment.'

'I never heard that!'

'Well, no one really talks about it . . . '

Robbie's gossip was notoriously fanciful. I put it out of my mind, together with the Ugliest Man. The local contracts had by now been negotiated and were passed to someone else for the routine stages, so I was no longer involved in municipal business. Besides, I got married at about that time and we took a flat in the suburbs from which, once home, I was reluctant to go out in the evenings. It was only when, with a second child on the way, we wanted a proper house and moved to P. . . that I saw him again. He was with Her.

They were at another table in the only decent restaurant. She was better dressed than in the old days, but the clothes still looked dowdy on her. I realized that I had been seeing her regularly ever since our move, because she worked in the baker's shop where they did rather good French bread that I often bought on my way home.

The next time I queued for my *baguette* I studied her closely. The years had not made as great an impact on her as on some people I knew, but then, she had been plain to start with. She had a slightly floury skin, which I had unthinkingly connected with the bakery. I now realized it was a rather tired skin; perhaps it had originally been too delicate to last – her mouse-coloured hair was consistent with that. She was unwrinkled, except for a few good-humour lines about her eyes and mouth. The eyes were ordinary and the mouth was getting blurred at the edges, but had not entirely lost the vulnerable pout of youth. When she smiled, which she obligingly did for every customer, she revealed that one molar was missing, leaving a just apparent and rather endearing gap. She seemed like any other contented suburban housewife, doing a light job in middle age, for pin-money or just to get out of the house. I did not always see her in the shop, so I supposed she worked part-time.

The restaurant turned out to be a favourite of the Ugliest Man and the woman. My wife liked it too, and so I often saw them together. I considered the possibility that their relationship was platonic – an intense friendship, possibly based on a love affair all those years ago. Perhaps she had not been free to marry then, and he had despaired and married someone else, but still their deep regard for each other continued . . . and so on. But I was not sure; some things did not fit. Usually they left the restaurant together, but once she had to go early. For a second, after he had helped her into her coat, he took her hand, then relinquished it with something of the old reluctance. That made me wonder.

So I was all the more surprised when, scarcely a week later, I saw him in town with another young girl. A very young girl. She was dressed differently from his secretaries – not more expensively, nor more carefully, but with more flair. She looked at him with open admiration, but at the same time treated him with a familiarity that the others did not venture. Above all, when he passed me after leaving her, I saw the same entranced expression on his face as I had seen so many years before, when he emerged from the underpass. I was, frankly, shocked. So much so that I followed the girl into a bookshop and studied her from the other side of a bookshelf. She was quite beautiful.

I was indignant. The next time I saw him in the restaurant I changed my place to avoid looking at him. The time after that the place was full and we were seated so that I could not help watching him. I caught my wife looking at me as I attacked my food vengefully at the sight of him creasing his face and smacking his blubber lips and making the woman, in her innocence, laugh so easily. I refused to look, and talked brightly about nothing in particular. Then my attention was caught by a slight but sudden movement at their table. The woman had raised herself in her place and was smiling eagerly as she waved to someone behind me. The man turned, and his awful features buckled in a seismic smile as well. Then I saw that they were both looking at the beautiful girl as she hurried across to them, even more delightful as, cheeks flushed with haste, she babbled excuses. She sat down at their table and the man leaned over and kissed her cheek.

I realized I had made a stupid mistake. I had forgotten how the years had passed. This must be – I looked from one to another of the animated faces and it was clear that the glorious young creature was the child of the other two. By that incomprehensible system by which children can resemble both their parents in every feature and yet be different from each of them, this radiant beauty was an amalgam of the insipid plainness and the gross ugliness that sat beside her. She resembled them both but she was like neither, in that she was beautiful and they were not.

'Whatever are you dreaming about?' asked my wife.

'Nothing,' I said, and told my first lie to her. It was to be expected, for I had just realized I was hopelessly involved with someone else.

The three of them went out laughing together and the crowded restaurant seemed almost empty. My wife looked after them as they passed the window, with something approaching longing, and I realized that she, too, was captivated.

A Delicate Nose

He closed on the woman, approaching, if not out of the sun, at least with the gallery spotlights behind him. When he was about a yard away and drawing breath to speak, she suddenly moved to the next picture. Then she took a step backwards, offering him a mass of black hair. Nonplussed, he studied the Modigliani she had vacated.

The girl on the canvas drooped – sleepily rather than sadly – on one raised shoulder. He explored the sun-ripened limbs, assessed the modest but adequate breasts – weighing the subtle relationships of tone and colour between each nipple and the surrounding skin – and passed to the gently formed belly and the double curve that described the plenitude of hips. Erotic, yes, but by no means a pin-up. More the rumination of a man with a vivid appetite for women and a habit of regular feeding. Lionel felt his own inadequacy.

And there it was again – unmistakably. He glanced sideways at the dark woman and breathed it: large and full, yet not at all sickly. He tried a few discreet sniffs, to get the top notes. The woman turned – for a moment he thought it was anxiety at his sniffing, but her passing glance was expressionless.

In fact she was heading for the exit. The Modigliani, still in the corner of his eye, emboldened him. One must enter the meadow if one is to pluck the flowers; he moved quickly and quietly.

'Excuse me,' he said.

The woman turned. Her face was quite young, but with well-defined features, and at the moment a startled expression borrowed from childhood.

'I don't want to seem impertinent,' Lionel began; the eyes widened slightly, and perhaps the lips tightened. He spoke faster: '– but I wonder if you'd mind telling me the name of the perfume you're wearing? You see, it's my wife's –'

'Oh.' Surprise became an embarrassed laugh. 'It's . . . .'

She lingered, eyes on a Bonnard where cool greens qualified mauve shadows and grey was sonorous beside dull cherry touched with scarlet. Then, in a low and slightly guttural voice she said, 'You know, I really don't have the name.'

'Ah, well . . . ' Lionel resigned himself to ignorance, and to the conclusion that he had been smoothly rebuked.

'I'm so sorry,' she said.

They both laughed. Yes, she laughed too, so perhaps she really couldn't remember. And she didn't switch off the laugh sharply, either, but smiled as she excused herself and turned to the lift.

After that the paintings seemed dull facsimiles of living reality and Lionel soon left the gallery too. He took the tube to Oxford Circus. Lazarus's was always his last resort for presents. The name on the wrapping, at least, would be all right. Now, his nose attuned, he went to the scent counter.

'I'm looking for a perfume – sort of resiny –'

He wanted to say 'with a rumour of spices and a descant of orange-blossom and a touch of spring larches', but instead he said '– sort of – you know – fruity.'

The milk-skinned girl who presided over trays of gilded flasks and frosted bottles under the sign 'French Perfumes' appeared to take him quite seriously.

'Well, we have *Scandale* . . . then, if it's for someone younger, there's *Zoum* . . .' She dabbled her long white fingers among the bottles of yellow and green liquids and offered a mauve drum and a shocking pink package.

Lionel hummed over them. 'I don't think it's either of those.'

'Is it for your wife?'

'Yes.'

'Is she very feminine?'

'Well . . . '

'If she's very feminine there's *Femme* – that's really heavy and very feminine.'

Lionel thought of fat fertility goddesses and looked doubtful.

'Or there's *Vent-Vert* – that's very green and fresh –' she glanced at Lionel '– but for a younger person, really. Then there's –'

'What about "*Y*"?'

Lionel pronounced it 'Ee', but wondered if he should have said – what was it? – 'Ee-grec'.

'Why?'

'I beg your pardon? – Oh, yes, of course – "Y".'

He sniffed the proffered wrist. There was a pleasant sheen on the tiny lozenge-shaped segments of skin and a flawlessly economical transition into lower arm.

'No-o, I don't think so.'

Then, clutching at a vaguely remembered advertisement: 'I wonder, have you got –' he hesitated a moment ' – "It"?'

'No, but there's "*De*" – that's very popular – or "*Le*" – that's new this season . . .' She dabbled among the bottles again. 'Then there's "*Oui*".'

Lionel floundered in monosyllables. Then he remembered his boldness in the gallery.

'What's that you're wearing?' he asked.

'Intimacy,' breathed the girl, and blushed. They both frowned at the elaborately modelled sprays, the square bottles with sham tortoise-shell tops and the flasks tied with bits of ribbon.

The madame in charge of the department gently elbowed the girl aside. She disciplined the bottles with fingers tipped with guardsmen's scarlet, and interrogated Lionel with a pursed smile. When he failed to respond she asked, 'What exactly were you looking for?'

'It's all right, thanks,' said Lionel, and left.

But there it was! He caught it drifting in the archway leading from perfume and stockings to leather and jewellery; evocative, sonorous and at the same time elated. He stepped through the arch and almost bumped into her where she stood before a display of gloves. She looked up, and as her glance passed

61

above his head to the illuminated 'perfumery' sign she smiled.

'Any luck?'

'Afraid not.'

They both laughed. She had good teeth.

As Lionel simpered and turned towards stockings and lingerie, she spoke again.

'Perhaps I can ask you something this time. Could you tell me where I can find a tie like yours?'

'Of course . . . ' But he had forgotten. They both laughed again and she was about to turn back to the gloves.

'Look,' he heard himself saying, 'we could have a cup of coffee – then we might both remember.'

The woman turned and looked at him deliberately, the ghost of a smile twitching her mouth. Lionel prepared to be snubbed.

'All right,' she said.

It was a moment before he could gather himself and say 'There's a place just round the corner' – a discreet teashop where old ladies gathered before looking for a taxi after shopping.

He led her away through jewellery, where Arabs consulted with bowed heads as they fingered ornate pieces, to the cool shock of the street. Shepherding her across he felt that light, amusing talk was required, but could think of nothing to say. Worse, when they reached the teashop he found it had become a kebab house emitting oniony smoke, and too late he remembered Lazarus's coffee-room a few yards from where they had started.

'It – seems to have changed,' he said.

'It's all right, I think they have coffee.'

'You really think so?'

'Yes, I think so,' and she led the way in. The smoke was confined to the street front and there was in fact a good smell of coffee. Lionel helped her with her coat; a pleasant narrowness of waist and fullness of hip was disclosed. They sat down. 'You know, I – ' they both began at once.

He gave her precedence.

'I was going to say that I don't do this sort of thing often,' she said.

Lionel, who had been about to explain that he didn't usually do this sort of thing, found the remark embarrassingly hackneyed. But on reflection the phrase 'this sort of thing' was promising; they were doing 'this sort of thing' . . . Who knew where it might lead?

'And I really can't tell you the name of the perfume,' she said. 'It was given to me abroad – it's brought from somewhere in the Caucasus, or perhaps beyond – India or China – on camels, I think. It isn't really commercial.'

Lionel hummed his interest. 'And I'm afraid the tie was a present,' he said. 'So I really don't know where it came from – but they do have quite a selection in Lazarus's.'

'But not quite what I wanted.'

Lionel bobbed his head in sympathy. 'Is it your Christmas shopping?'

'More or less. And yours?'

'Birthday, really,' Lionel thought of Jenny and felt awkward. 'Have you spent much time in the East?' he asked.

She laughed. 'Well – it's a bit complicated.'

Best not to enquire further, then. It was quite natural that she might not want to go into her background, especially as it might involve discussing embarrassingly personal relationships. He wondered, though. Perhaps she was a colonial service child, though the accent was not Anglo-Indian chi-chi. French, perhaps – married, or a mistress; the status symbol of some complaisant oil potentate.

They drank the thick coffee that had come in a little brass saucepan on a tray with two tiny cups like miniature handle-less chamber-pots. Lionel groped for conversation. He had a childish impulse to play safe and escape before the whole thing became embarrassing, but he knew he would be furious with himself afterwards if he did. He took a breath and, not looking at her face, but studying the slim, bony fingers with which she decanted second cups, deftly keeping back most of the dregs, he said:

'If you've finished your shopping we could have lunch.'

Surprised, she laughed again, and looked at him appraisingly. 'I'm sorry,' he said. 'It's just that – well, since I've approached a stange woman for the first time in years I really feel I ought to make the most of it.' Was that the right thing to say?

'You make it sound like a painful duty!'

'Not at all – I mean, I should – '

'– But it's not possible, I'm afraid. I have to meet someone.' With rueful cheerfulness Lionel conceded. Thank God, he had done all that retrospect could require of him.

But what was this? He froze as he heard her saying, quietly and evenly: 'If you would like to come round for a drink this evening I'm at Maugham's in Half Moon Street.'

His astonishment must have been obvious, but as she stood up she added smoothly, 'About six?'

Lioned stammered that he'd love to, and scrambled to his feet too late to help her with her coat. As she dismissed his fluttering hands and quickly buttoned it at throat and waist she said: 'I'm sorry. I really must rush. Six o'clock at Maugham's, then – ask at the desk for "Noor" – N-double-o-r.'

And in a delicious flurry of that perfume she was gone.

Lionel rejected the idea of eating a kebab, went back to Lazarus's and bought Jenny a very extravagant nightdress. Naturally, he thought about his assignation all the time, and continued to do so while he ate a pasta. It was true that he hadn't done this sort of thing for years – well, ever, really.

'Come round for a drink . . . ' – he checked that he had enough money on him – and after that? What exactly did she have in mind? 'Ask at the desk' – did that mean that she was inviting him to her room? He found he had finished his lasagne with total inattention.

In Foyle's he again constructed her possible background. She was obviously a decent, serious sort of woman – out of the question to fit her into a scenario of vice or blackmail. Perhaps a bored wife, proving she was real by an *acte gratuit* and just as scared as he was? The chances were that the whole thing would come down to a rather difficult half-hour on uncomfortable bar-stools, struggling to make conversation. At worst, she simply wouldn't turn up.

To kill time he went to the cinema, where for once he felt himself an equal of the privileged beings on the screen, living in a world as charged with passion and adventure as the one in which they mooned and glowered.

At ten to six he found the hotel and approached the reception desk, dodging a porter who was heaving a cabin trunk about the foyer with cheerful fury.

'I'm look for a Miss – a lady called "Noor" – N-double-o-r,' he said.

'Just a moment, Sir . . . ' The receptionist hitched his glasses and ran a pencil down the columns of the register. 'I don't recall that name,' he said, turning back the page and continuing to skim the signatures.

So that was that, Lionel decided.

'There's a Mr Norris in two-three-one,' offered the receptionist.

Lionel rejected Mr Norris.

'I'm afraid I can't help you then, sir.' The receptionist looked up. His 'No sir!' had a final ring.

'Do you mind if I wait a few minutes?'

The receptionist, who had already turned to a pair of Arabs, waved permission. 'Suit yourself, sir – seat over there,' and he attended to the robed figures and their confidential gaspings.

So he had been 'stood up'. Perhaps she had panicked at the last moment, or perhaps she had been pulling his leg all the time. The first was the more agreeable, but the second the more likely explanation. He would give it ten minutes and then put the whole business down to experience.

As he strolled the width of the foyer he broodingly watched a young couple that had just come in. The girl playfully ruffled the boy's hair before squeezing his arm and sending him across to the reception desk. Lionel passed near her, and she smelt nice – but a bit obvious. He lingered by the umbrella stand for a minute or two and then strolled back. The young man returned from the desk and after a joyful reunion the couple hurried to the lift. Meanwhile the two Arabs had emerged from sour contemplation to greet a third with low rasping sounds.

It was time to go. At the doorway Lionel met the porter locked in jovial conflict with a suitcase.

And there it was! Faint but unmistakable. The gust of cold air from outside sharpened the spicy fragrance and Lionel stood for a moment, to catch its last vestige. He took two steps back into the foyer, and there it was again – and by the lift, where the suitcase now lay after the porter's *coup de grâce*.

The suitcase – that must be her suitcase! Lionel caught the scent again as he looked for a name in the little leather tag by the handle, but found none. He straightened up and watched the door, expecting a slim figure. A slight noise from the direction of the suitcase made him turn round . . .

The bomb was quite small. It devastated the foyer, stunned the receptionist, blew the porter out through the door on to his back in the middle of the road, where he lay chuckling inanely, blew arms and legs off the three Arabs, and killed Lionel instantly.

At eight o'clock Melissa finished her *filet*. It was excellent, though it would have been even better with wine – pity Nassim was so strict. He had been on edge throughout the meal, too, waiting for news. Now he came back from the telephone, nodding and winking in his well-cut suit that still looked tight across his soldier's shoulders.

'Perfect!' he said, as he sat down. 'Three Saudis and a local.' He smiled at her.

Melissa smiled back. It had been easy, as always.

Nassim spoke more gently – even indulgently, for she had been a good girl: 'Did you do your shopping?'

'Oh, yes.' She reached down to her leather shoulder-bag and rummaged a moment. 'And I forgot to give you this.'

He laughed, and undid the package with a generous show of enthusiasm, then he held the tie to his throat and posed for her. The colour looked even better on him than on that pestering English fool this morning, and she was glad she had persisted

until she had found it, in Simpson's. She wondered if the
Englishman had kept his appointment, and suppressed a giggle
– Nassim might think she was laughing at him, and that always
caused trouble. Now she leaned back, looking at his handsome
cropped head as he ordered coffee; missing a cigarette, but
breathing her own perfume that she loved so much.

'It's funny,' she said. 'This perfume – does it really come in
camel caravans?'

Nassim laughed. 'Lorries, actually. It comes with the
explosive – it's a sort of by-product.'

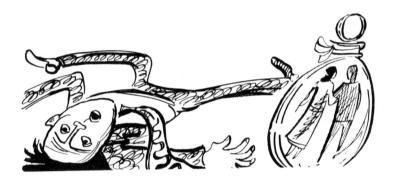

Mr Parsley's Lunchtime Pursuit

Did Mr Parsley have any inkling when he entered the pub? Outside was the slabby, carpentered mahogany that might have seen the world of before 1914, or could equally have dated from the 1950s. The lettering above the arched windows was reassuringly conventional and the windows themselves were curtained in some sort of plush. In the lobby, before he pushed open the door, Mr Parsley heard thumping music. The noise engulfed him as he stepped inside on to the grey plank floor where men stood, holding glasses to their chests and all facing one way with quizzically indulgent expressions on their faces.

Of course, Mr Parsley had a very good inkling. He had confirmed the promise of the curtained windows by checking that the darkness at the edges of the plush fluctuated rhythmically as if lights were flashing inside, and he had paused before opening the swing doors to ensure that, although there was loud music, there was not much conversational hubbub. His scanning of the customers as he pushed open the door was also purposeful – if they had been facing in all directions, talking and drinking, he would have let the door swing shut again, and gone elsewhere.

The first time he really hadn't known. It had been in the bar across the road. He had been sipping a half-pint, annoyed by the music and puzzled by the atmosphere of expectancy. The patch of coloured light projected on to one wall, in which a succession of magazine images appeared to be filtered through a bubble-bath, he had taken for a piece of tawdry decoration that came with the juke-box.

He had drunk his beer with increasing distaste, suspecting, then confirming, that the glass was tainted with onion. Those damned crisps! As he frowned along the sides of the glass he noticed a pair of female ankles by the juke-box and, when the drinkers on that side of the room shifted in their talk, he dully observed the back of a pair of slim knees and a surprising extent of stockinged thigh. The thighs shifted as weight was transferred from one to another, and Mr Parsley stared over his beer at dimpled buttocks, saved from complete exposure by a chevron of black knicker. The buttocks were then veiled and unveiled, veiled and unveiled several times by a fringed shawl that – Mr Parsley had craned to see – depended from arms that were busy putting money in the juke-box.

The girl turned, with a dismissive smile at whatever the middle-aged man had said to her through his eager false teeth, sprang on to a dais, and began to twist and convulse to the music while the circle of coloured light played its pink and lilac bubble-bath over her torso.

Mr Parsley had found it rather embarrassing at first. He had looked at the other customers, but they were all intent on the figure on the dais, except for one man who deliberately turned away to speak to his glassy-eyed neighbour. Turning away like that struck Mr Parsley as rude, and he conscientiously returned his own attention to the dancer. She was mouthing the words of the juke-box song, her eyes wandering absently round the room. Her gaze met Mr Parsley's and stayed on him for a moment as she mouthed 'Baby love oh, baby love! . . .' Mr Parsley smiled nervously and shifted his attention as soon as he could from her face to the less intimate ground of twisting flanks and swaying hips

When the record stopped the girl stood waiting while the juke-box clicked and whirred. The men who had been watching so intently suddenly remembered their beer and conversations and ignored her. When the music started up again, so did she, twisting and writhing to a slower rhythm. She ran her hands down her own body with an expression of rapt appreciation; she turned round and bent over, looking between her legs at the audience as she solemnly waved her backside at them like a priest elevating the Host before his congregation. Towards the end of the third record she removed her brassière, and Mr Parsley found himself refreshed by the sight of a simple body, no longer tricked out in teasing scraps. But it seemed rather vulnerable, and he preferred to watch it in the mirror that carried a gilt advertisement for India Pale Ale.

Since that first time Mr Parsley had regularly sought out pubs with 'live entertainment'. He soon gave up pretending that he only chose them by accident, or that what really interested him was observing the audience. Mr Parsley knew that he came, like all the others, to look at the girls. He had his preferences – of type, not individual, for he seldom cared to see the same girl twice. Ponderous hips swaying under a 'shortie' nightie were not for him. And once a girl with a splendid figure, dancing very gracefully on bare feet, put him off completely because she so clearly resented having to earn money that way and had such evident contempt for the men who came to watch her. Mr Parsley stayed to the end only because she was so beautiful and he wanted to see her take off her bra – as they usually did. But she had stepped contemptuously down from the platform without doing so.

He was happiest when the girl herself seemed to enjoy what she was doing – even if it was only gyrating vacuously to the music – and especially if she struck up a relationship with the audience, making sharp comments and taking obvious pleasure in their admiration. Once or twice Mr Parsley was afraid some spirited girl might single him out for teasing, but that never happened. They seemed to know who to go for.

Nowadays Mr Parsley liked to follow his lunchtime pursuit with a certain discrimination and subtlety – it helped maintain the interest. If he had time, he liked to arrive before the dancing began and to size up the girl as she took a preliminary drink at the bar. That way he could discreetly slip out if she was raddled, or overblown or vulgar. He never liked to leave while a performance was in progress because that seemed insulting, and he didn't like to leave immediately afterwards because that suggested that he only came to gloat – in a way he did, of course, but not lustfully. With him it was a matter of aesthetic pleasure in trim young bodies – wonderful for the figure, all that dancing – rather than prurient curiosity. After all, he always looked away if the performance became too suggestive.

Today again, he played the mirror trick. You couldn't do that everywhere, but it added interest and made it easier to slip out unnoticed if need be. When he entered the bar he did not allow himself to look directly at the dancer, but stayed behind a square pillar just inside the door and watched in the old-fashioned mirror with its advertisement for some forgotten ale. He could see the girl between the gilt lettering, pretty well unimpeded from just below the neck to just above the knees; a palely radiant figure against the dark panelling of the bar, skin lightly tanned against the all-white stockings and suspenders. Mr Parsley thought the white rather nice – much better than the black with puce trimmings that was usually considered 'sexy'. Clean, too. The darting arrows of the suspender-belt and the stockings that contrasted so flatteringly with warm skin-tones were impeccable. Mr Parsley liked that.

He was curious to see her face – she must be a new girl – but he teased himself by accepting what the mirror showed him: now thorax and thighs, separated by marching gilt letters; now undulant hips, wriggling between the lines. The swaying figure turned round and Mr Parsley admired the long, sweet curve of a back, then looked away when the girl straddled her legs and bent down. He did not want it not to be nice. But when he looked back the mirror was empty. He peered round the pillar and over the heads in front of him – he had to stand on tiptoe, for everyone was craning – and caught sight of a pair of upturned legs; she must be lying on her back. Admirable musculature played on fine bones. Mr Parsley enjoyed the slow drawing off of a pair of white stockings.

The record stopped, and Mr Parsley subsided behind his pillar. At this point the normal sounds of the bar usually asserted themselves. But this time there was no bleeping from the Space Invaders, no cascade of coins from the fruit machine, and only subdued conversation. This girl was good. Mr Parsley liked these signs of appreciation where it was due. It showed that the ordinary man had discernment after all.

The next record started and the girl reappeared in the mirror.

She was dancing with unusual originality, thrusting a hip at the audience and wagging it provocatively, then swaying back with the light flowing and ebbing over her flat belly. Eventually her torso – still all that Mr Parsley could see of her – arched as she reached behind to unhook her brassière. It was really such a wholesome body; to Mr Parsley there seemed to be an inevitability about its rounded forms and way of moving – a familiarity, almost, though he was sure he had never seen this dancer before.

He bent his head and peered into the top half of the mirror, trying to catch her face as she undulated, the scrap of lace across her breasts supported only by pressed arms against ribs in mock coyness while her head was flung back in sham ecstasy. Between the gilt letters the pale oval of face dodged and swayed. The lips breathed the lyric of the record through a knowing half-smile. Mr Parsley blinked to brush away the illusion that – Oh Lord!

The girl had raised her head and the half-closed eyes had suddenly opened wide to stare into the mirror straight at him. For a second the cherry mouth froze, gaping wider than the 'o' of 'love' demanded. The gyrating hips jerked fitfully, then stopped, like failing machinery. As the record faded her gasp was audible throughout the bar.

'Dad!'

Her arms had jerked from her sides, fingers stiffened as if to plunge at her own body. The unsupported brassière fell to the ground. A half-naked teenager, she stared round the room looking for Mr Parsley.

Stepan

The island was very poor. It was made of the same grey-white rock that had been shipped across the Adriatic to build Venice. Now the stony slopes supported flocks of hook-nosed, long-legged sheep and a human population that smiled too little to be Italian – though the Lion of St Mark still paced on several gateways, the old people still spoke Italian between themselves, and the iron bollards round the harbour murmured through a layer of rust that they were cast in Bologna.

There was very little for the young men to do on the island. Some found work on the ferries or the jetty, or doing the heavy jobs at the cannery. A contingent marshalled by Milovan, the ex-partisan, were still finishing the holiday village that stood empty further down the bay. The rest fished for sardines or watched sheep. Of course, in summer everyone watched the tourists.

The season began, not very convincingly, with a few Italian families bringing caravans for the Easter weekend. Then motorcycles, dusty after the long run from Bavaria and beyond, came throbbing and weaving along the path to the campsite. The riders wore Zapata moustaches and a day's stubble under their windowed helmets. Each was clutched round the loins by a girl in a zipper suit that glistened tautly over her hips. They put up diminutive tents, smoked, and strummed guitars. When they had rested they crawled into the tents and, doubtless, made love.

The bikes were followed by the cars: big Mercedes brimming with families, and coupés containing debonair couples. Still later other couples came bouncing in Citroëns and Renaults. The Mercedes tourists distributed themselves between the hotel and the campsite – usually couples to the hotel and families to the campsite, where they put up big frame tents with little fences and bowls of fruit on tables. The Citroëns and Renaults disgorged tents scarcely bigger than those of the motorcyclists. Apart from the odd patched wigwam, with a middle-aged English couple stewing baked beans in the dust outside, it was the little tents that were worth watching.

Stepan, a bookkeeper at the cannery, once crept into the camp at night and held his breath as he listened to the crescendo of sighs from a tiny tent that floundered in the moonlight beside an enormous motorcycle. When there came the bang and hiss of a deflating air-bed and the sighs dissolved into helpless giggles he had slunk away in a turmoil, and at home his mother had scolded him for slamming the door so hard that a tray had fallen down and broken two glasses.

It was not that there were no women in the village. In fact there were more women than men, but half of them were widows. They, and most of the other women over forty, wore black. Young matrons marked their status by a degree of soberness in dress. The unmarried girls – those that hadn't left for the mainland – walked out on the quayside in standard floral dresses from the mainland shops, or badly cut jeans. But the tourist women sunbathed in bikinis, monokinis, or nothing. That was why the men watched them.

The most convenient observation ground was the path between the stony olive terraces and the shore. It was separated from the water's edge by a band of coarse shingle with occasional flat rocks suitable for sunbathing. In places there was a broken screen of pines and cypresses. The tourists emerged each morning and distributed themselves on the rocks. The boys patrolled the path, watching them, and in summer Milovan led his gang out to the tourist village, not by the direct path through the trees, but along the beach path. They, too, watched the tourists – but rather crudely, greeting the most indiscreet couples with a cheerful bellow as they passed. It tended to spoil the pitch for more subtle observers.

The boys watched mainly at weekends. Josip, who earned good money maintaining machinery in the harbour, whirred up and down on a motorized bicycle. He covered most ground, but his visions were fleeting. Besides, no matter how fast he rode, his appearance was never entirely a surprise. The others strolled, usually in pairs. A few – among them the most dedicated – hunted alone. Stepan was one of those. He came whenever he could.

Sunday was a good day, but he was usually delayed by having to accompany his mother to church. As they came out with the other old ladies, after the service, he would say that he wanted a breath of air and hurry off, breaking into a run as soon as he was out of sight. He would run through the campsite and along the first part of the beach path, but when he came to the sunbathing rocks he slowed to a walk. Somehow he never acquired the knack of strolling casually. Since he had no companion he couldn't stop, engrossed in conversation, facing out to sea but watching a rock from the corner of his eye – in any case, his glasses would have made that difficult. Instead, he walked quickly, with short nervous steps, and stopped to look frankly at what interested him. There were several embarrassing misunderstandings. If he had got on better with the other boys they would have shown him how to be less conspicuous – and have pointed out that his white shirt was a mistake for a start. But Stepan did not join easily in the knowing, nudging conversations at the tables outside the harbour café – though the stories told by Jovan, who worked part-time at the hotel, were fascinating. Stepan only half believed them, of course, but he knew it was certainly true that the tourists could behave badly.

For instance, early in the summer he was keeping observation on a young couple who had camped at the site without the benefit of a tent. He had monitored the motionless bulk of their sleeping-bags under the olives until late at night, and the next day he had hurried down before work, just in time to see them disappearing towards the beach. He hung about for a few minutes, then followed. As he emerged on to the shore he caught the gleam of bare skin on the rocks. The boy was standing to spread a towel. The girl was already lying on one, her long flanks unbroken by any garment.

A moment later Stepan was bitterly disappointed to see her sit up and pull on a pair of shorts. As he came nearer he saw why. An angler – a tourist – had settled on the next flat stone, but he had abandoned his rod and, vaguely pretending to adjust the socks that hung round his scaly mauve ankles, had settled down to stare at the girl's candid body, lechery patent in his blotched face.

Stepan was indignant. One didn't expect that sort of behaviour from tourists. Now the girl saw him standing there too, and at this last straw she flopped on to her stomach and flattened her arms to her sides. Stepan hurried by, hating the German fisherman. Round the corner he found the man's wife, picking flowers in a diminutive sun-frock. From beneath it her legs emerged like uncooked sausages and from above it, with a heave of pink neck, she turned on him the face of an aging male member of the Politburo. Stepan found his anger gone.

Other hazards were of a more natural sort. Sometimes people would place themselves directly under the rim of the path, invisible unless one descended to the rocks oneself. Stepan was reluctant to leave the path and preferred to hang about above, stalking the occasional emergent foot and craning his neck to trace a leg to its source in a triangle of gay cotton or expanse of reddening skin.

One couple interested him particularly. He followed them, but had to feign indifference and look out to sea while Josip whined by, jeering, on his wobbling motorized bike. He looked back, but the quarry had vanished. He had liked her cool cotton skirt and the tee-shirt with an apple printed on the front. Yesterday, from a stance near the harbour, he had seen the apple plumpen as a hand slid under it. She had smiled as she gently disengaged herself. Now they had come looking for a more discreet spot for plucking apples, and he had lost them! After work he saw them again, strolling contentedly back to the hotel. She carried her skirt in her bag, and looked smug and sunburnt as her tiny costume jived about her hips.

The next day Stepan was sitting throwing pebbles at the sea before Milovan led his troop of workers out. He waited, ignoring the occasional early bathers who passed along the path. An Italian family came to a flat rock nearby. The children played in the shingle; the father began to fish and the mother sunbathed. Her fair hair was in a pony-tail that tossed as she arranged her towel before lying down. She seemed very young and Stepan wondered what she had been like before she had those children. He glared at the father and threw pebbles with greater vehemence. When he looked back at the mother he found she had discarded the top of her costume and two breasts were offered to the sun. Stepan devoured their golden symmetry. The husband looked at him in sharp enquiry, but Stepan's eyes which, even while feasting had kept flickering occasionally to the left, had caught sight of a skirt and tee-shirt, coming bright through the olives. He studied a pebble, and heard their feet, gentle on the path behind, and caught a drift of her laughter. He waited a few more minutes then, with a final gulp at the warm rotundities before him, he set off on the day's main business.

He hurried along the path, looking anxiously through the glaucous olives. Then he relaxed his pace, disappointed at finding the striped skirt demurely settled on a rock. The girl, still wearing it, was dabbling her feet in the water. The man was smoking a cigarette. Stepan passed them resentfully, regretting the Italian family. Round the corner he disconsolately watched a man bathing naked – the thought of exposing oneself like that!

The man came out of the water and walked over to where his towel lay. He saw Stepan staring and said something to him, sharply, in a foreign language. Stepan made no reply and the man shrugged, wrapped the towel round his middle, crossed the path and clambered up the rocks. He pulled on some shorts and settled down before what looked like a canvas on an easel. Stepan watched. The man looked down at him, then became engrossed in his work. Stepan walked on a little, then returned to watch again. Finally he went a little further along the path, climbed up into the rocks and made his way back through the olives to a point behind the painter.

The picture was a bright blur of colour. Stepan descended to look more closely. The man heard the stones clattering and looked round. Stepan nodded. The man sighed and turned back to his easel. Stepan watched from over his shoulder. Presently the man spoke, in an Italian worse than Stepan's. He asked about the village, and what Stepan did. Stepan replied in near-monosyllables. The man asked if more tourists would come. Stepan said there would be many – nudists too – he made his disapproval clear and felt his lip curl. All the nudists would be tourists, said Stepan – not people from the village. The man grunted and dabbed at his canvas. Then he leaned back in appraisal. What would such a picture cost? asked Stepan. The man shrugged. Stepan suggested five hundred dinars; he had seven hundred in a wallet at home. The man laughed and began to paint again. Perhaps five hundred was too much. Stepan did not pursue the point, but watched as the bright paste was stabbed and stirred on the palette and dabbed on to the canvas. It seemed a more agreeable occupation than bookkeeping.

The he saw them pass by on the path below. The striped skirt swayed as she walked and the yellow hair swung as she laughed. They disappeared and Stepan forced himself to wait a little. It would not do to follow too closely. The painter spoke again, asking some question or other. Stepan made a vaguely affirmative sound. He had seen them again, where the path re-emerged with the curve of the shore. They were passing the holiday village and going further on. As they disappeared a second time Stepan stood up.

'*Arrivederci*,' said the painter.

'*Dovidjenia*,' muttered Stepan, and clattered down the rocks.

He reached the tourist village and crossed the new section of concrete path in front of it. The old beach path resumed on the other side. There were more trees here, and occasional walls descended at right angles to the sea, with wattle gates to keep the sheep. Stepan approached each barrier with caution, but no one was on the other side. He paused by the shepherd's hut, scanning the little cove that lay below it – a likely spot – but no bright cotton drew his eye. He began to think he must have missed them where the trees hid the beach. He hurried on impatiently, and then he saw them, a few yards away on the other side of the little bay where the old mooring post stood. They were naked, and making love.

Stepan made no attempt to conceal himself but stood in elated disapproval, staring at these bodies whose movements, now languorous, now urgent, were so strangely dignified. Afterwards the sun laid a segment of rainbow along the man's wet back. The rainbow broke as the back flexed and the man looked up to see Stepan. He started, then quickly got to his feet, nonplussed for a moment. The girl still lay in contented nudity. The man spoke sharply to Stepan, who glanced at him for a moment, then looked back at the girl, who had now seen him and had drawn her discarded skirt over her lap as she sat up in surprise. The man spoke again, and approached a step or two, but Stepan was absorbed in the way the slight breasts moved, the shoulder curved and the hip flexed in its fullness.

The man shouted. Stepan looked at him and tried to speak, but his mouth was dry and only a husky croak emerged. Suddenly the man laughed. Still laughing, he turned to the girl and indicated Stepan. The girl's posture of embarrassment relaxed a little, and her startled mask broke with rueful humour. The man turned back to Stepan, made an elaborate bow and extended a hand, then swept it towards the girl in a gesture of lordly invitation. The girl laughed and looked doubtfully, then boldly, at Stepan. Stepan was uncomprehending for a moment, then his mind flooded with understanding.

The girl gave the alarm at the hotel. She had run past the surprised sunbathers and through the campsite without stopping, her honking sobs and tee-shirt wet with tears at odds with her jaunty bikini pants. She choked out her story of the struggle and the blood only when she reaching the reassuring world of carpets and reception desks.

The local policeman came and clambered ineffectually over the rocks in the hot afternoon. Then the superintendent arrived, confidently half-smiling in his snappy blouse and cap. He organized a sweep of the olives that quickly flushed out the miscreant, who was taken, stumbling in handcuffs, to the mainland.

The case was a delicate one. It was important that the tourists should not be discouraged, but fortunately there was no suggestion of sexual assault. In court the girl told her story yet again, exactly as she had done at the hotel, at the police station and at the procurator's office. She described the boy's sudden appearance, how he had turned to run away, had stumbled and blundered into 'that big stone' (the old bollard by the shore) and how, as if cornered, he had turned and . . . At that point she always became incoherent, but the forensic evidence – the description of the smashed skull, and the rock that lay, darkly stained, on the courtroom table – was clear enough.

The accused refused to give evidence, which was convenient, but not in his favour. There was testimony that he had not associated well with his fellow workers; there were lengthy psychiatric reports, and he was eventually consigned to a mental hospital for an indefinite period. Island gossip had its own version of the affair: a local lad in the coils of a brazen foreign woman was discovered by a jealous lover who under-estimated island mettle. That version surprised Stepan's mother, but it was the one she preferred to believe.

The girl returned to her job in Stuttgart and recovered from the incident surprisingly well. It had all happened between two plane-rides in the parenthetic world of holiday. It wasn't as if she had known Rudi for long. The image that troubled her most – that for a long time would suddenly flash across the paper in her typewriter – was of the moment when the boy spat on her body as he turned away from killing her friend.

Memories of Colonialism

I The Bight of Benin

Travel, like chickens, had a little more flavour in the 1950s – provided you were not someone important, like a Minister, or perishable, like a girl secretary, and that you did not have the misfortune to be a businessman whose time was his firm's money. Such people flew. For the rest of us it was not yet a matter of a few hours in a sealed cylinder of aeroplane and a few minutes blinking on another, sunnier airport, before arriving at an hotel kept at European temperature and staffed with foreign menials just like the one we had left in London. We still travelled.

Johnson was not important, perishable or in business. His journey to Africa began thirteen days before it ended; on a wet night in Liverpool when his ship jostled the last pier and he watched a girl – she afterwards turned out to be a mature woman and rather plain – hanging out of a porthole and waving goodbye to the Last of England in the persons of two longshoremen who obligingly waved back. The next morning dolphins wallowed in the pale scar the ship's passage left across the belly of the sea. Then there were blustery Biscay days with hot broth on deck at mid-morning and sad figures huddled by the rail. Warmth came suddenly, when the sun burst from behind clouds and stayed, beaming on a transformed sea – and a transformed ship.

There was swimming by day, dancing by night and vari-coloured long drinks with esoteric names at all times. Then there was the first sight of a green palm strand with clustered corrugated-iron roofs, and the first trip ashore to a world of black faces. And now, on its third and final landfall, the ship was entering a drab river-mouth. The bright atmosphere of the sea was gone; the dull water was streaked with oilstains. They were approaching a sultry, sweating shore of warehouses, some tall buildings and a low horizon of shacks. There was an atmosphere of used Saturday afternoons.

'The Bight of Benin, the Bight of Benin, there's few that's come out though there's many gone in,' intoned the ship's doctor.

A man from the department of which Johnson was now a junior official had come with a car to meet him. The pale figure wore blue shorts and a white shirt with a tie – none of the khaki bush-gear Johnson had foolishly expected – and radiated dullness. They drove down steaming streets on seats wet with sweat. Johnson, searching eagerly for signs of pulsing tropical life, could find excitement only in the windscreen-wipers, slapping to and fro with the desperation of bodies copulating. He should never have left the pale but willing girls of England for this.

'Read the files,' they said at the office. He dozed over them, only occasionally shocked awake by the more exciting items, such as the Special Arrangements for the Consignment of Groundnuts to Nigerian Workers in Fernando Po. He stapled together sheets of minutes prepared in advance of meetings at which African representatives would ratify the Administration's decisions. At night he returned to the guest house, which reminded him vividly of India, where he had never been.

Johnson was eager to 'experience' Africa – the real Africa that he supposed must underlie the city of big stores, where rich black people in European clothes selected refrigerators and gramophones and three-piece suites. He prowled along back-streets, tracking down drums that always turned into throbbing generators or men hammering petrol-cans out flat. Once a musical tinkling led him to where a group of happy tailors had abandoned their sewing machines to snip a rhythm out of the air with flashing scissors.

He peered at the stalls where soap and cola nuts were spread out for sale, lit by little lamps made from condensed milk tins. He breathed the dramatic stench of the gutters. He borrowed a bicycle and pedalled out over Carter Bridge to Yabba, where the office clerks lived. Beyond there the forest came down to the road, but it was not proper jungle; not vividly green, nor noticeably steaming. He had himself punted about the delta in a canoe, and was scolded for picking a coconut – for he had not yet learned, as everyone in the tropics must learn, that every coconut palm in the world belongs to someone.

He was invited to curry lunches and was cheered when he saw, over the shoulder of a fair-haired secretary with her back to the window, palm wine tapsters climbing like insects up hundred-foot trunks. But he was soon recalled to some story about the stupidity of servants.

He walked in the evening with a Scottish accountant, and admired the pale limbs of an African girl in a yellow dress who passed like a wavering candle though the dusk.

'Prostitute,' said the accountant, with satisfaction. The girl was followed by a shadowy figure: 'That's her keeper.'

Johnson envied the keeper.

'They don't get much out of it,' said the accountant.

'Out of what?'

'Sex, of course. They're not like us. They don't get much out of it at all,' said the accountant, with iron determination. Then he added, 'You need a hobby here, you know. Otherwise you go daft.'

The daftest thing Johnson did was to consult an oracle.

II Ifa and Mrs Director

The oracle lived in one of the maze of streets behind the big stores in the middle of town. Johnson went to see him on the borrowed bicycle, a fine upstanding machine, proud with polish and with pedals neatly encased and fringed with red rubber from inner-tubes. That was for the benefit of bare feet, and it served to remind Johnson that a white man riding a bicycle was odd. He pedalled past the big stores, survived the whirlpool of traffic in Tinubu Square and escaped along earthen Okepopo Street, where the dust was suppressed by the urine of flocks of goats and children. In some of the side streets taxis were parked beside the wrecks of their ancestors. But even African taxis could not penetrate those streets whose ends were crossed by the trenches of storm-drains. Johnson dragged the bike into one of them and considered directions.

'Where are you going, Mr Johnson?'

The gateman from the office was there, standing before his own door, his drab uniform replaced by a bright cloth hitched round his middle. He grinned his pleasure at being able to put a name to this European who was entertaining the street. Johnson explained.

'Oho! I think it is down there. Yes, that way. So long, Mr Johnson!'

Johnson got back on the bicycle and wobbled through the small crowd that had gathered. As he went he heard the gateman explaining that his colleague was riding a bicycle for exercise – he knew him well 'though he is but newly arrived among us'.

Soon Johnson had to ask again. The man he chose stared blankly, but another swaggered out of the shade.

'What do you want? Oracle? Not here please!' That was a statement, not a command. 'The Priest of Ifa? Oho! You want Chief Obafemi. Through there.'

A small boy tugged at Johnson's trousers and scampered ahead. He turned to see if Johnson was following and fell over an old woman's calabashes, then ran on, leaving Johnson to avoid the cries and spilt dinner as best he could. Everyone stopped to watch as they went by, and children squatting in the dirt bleated 'N'yeahbo, n'yeahbo' at the white man. The boy stopped and pointed to a board that said this was where Chief O. O. Obafemi specialized in womb troubles. Johnson gave him sixpence and carefully locked the borrowed bicycle.

In the compound Johnson explained what he wanted to a succession of young men. Each 'Ohoed' his understanding and fetched another, until the last led Johnson across the courtyard to a plank hut. The Chief was coming.

The inside of the hut was pale green. The floor and walls leaned one way, but the ceiling compensated by sagging the other. A chair was brought and Johnson sat before a low platform on which was a box covered with a cloth surmounted by a chair with a cushion. He was joined by an old man, a sort of chamberlain, who told him that the Chief was coming. A series of women arrived, some with babies, some heavily pregnant, and the hut began to take on the air of a doctor's waiting room. Presently a youth came in, to announce again that the Chief was coming. They waited; Johnson simpered at the chamberlain, who simpered back. At last the Chief arrived, sucking morsels of food from his teeth.

He was dressed in a white robe and carried a cowtail fly-switch. He was older than the chamberlain and moved very deliberately. Johnson took the glistening, almost reptilian hand that was offered him. Then the Chief went to his precarious throne, carefully climbed it, and sat down. He and Johnson nodded to each other, and a young man translated Johnson's account of why he was there.

– The white man wished to consult the oracle? Then he should wait till the women were dealt with.

One of them drank a dark mixture that evidently tasted awful, and handed over several banknotes. One exhibited her baby and received advice with sad noddings, and another gave thanks, bending to the floor. Then it was Johnson's turn.

The Chief slowly clambered down from his throne and came to sit facing him. He mumbled long incantations and repeatedly touched Johnson's brow and chest; he seemed to be cajoling the deity into having dealings with this oddity. Then one of the young men brought a cushion bearing a chain with spoon-like links. The old man took it, muttered over it, then tossed it like a dice. Peering at the way the links lay he drew marks with his fingers on a carved board. Then he thrust some beans into Johnson's surprised fists, and took them back again with a fierce plucking motion that made it a matter of chance whether he secured them all at once. Cowry shells were obscurely manipulated, dealt to Johnson, and taken back. It all reminded him of when someone had tried to teach him poker. Finally, the pronouncement:

'Yes.'

That was awkward, because Johnson had no particular question in mind. He explained his difficulty to the young man who, after a muttered conversation with the Chief, offered the supplementary interpretation that the white man was going on a journey. That was a safe bet about any government officer. Johnson still looked expectant, and the young man helped out with an assurance that he would soon be a big boss. Then the Chief spoke again. The white man must beware of woman. Especially the boss's woman, who could bring trouble.

That, too, was a safe bet.

And there was another woman . . .

Johnson shuffled in anticipation. What was she like?

'She is lying down,' said the Chief, primly. 'She is bigger trouble.'

It was, at least, intriguing.

There followed a blessing, involving porridge. For an awful moment Johnson thought he was going to have to eat the muck, but he was only daubed with it. No one laughed. He paid five shillings and left.

Next week Johnson was sent north, to the arid Moslem country that faded into the Sahara. He found vultures sitting on all the roofs and dry heat beating down from a flawless sky in which more vultures, reduced almost to specks, slowly planed and circled. The new office was more homely than the one in the capital. The Director's wife even helped with the typing, while they waited for a new girl to arrive. The Director's wife, sharp-breasted and lean, bestowed a twinkle here and a waggish look there. With her trip-down-the-scale laugh she admitted to having 'been out nineteen months this tour already, though I hope I don't look it.' Johnson, unkindly, thought she did.

At the end of his first week the Director's wife, all teeth, tits and dark glasses, hailed him as he was leaving the office. Could he run her home? The Director was on tour.

Of course! Johnson was delighted at the opportunity of showing off his new car. Then he remembered his appointment for a driving-licence photograph – without it he wasn't really legal. He started to explain that he had an appointment in the *Sabon Gari* (the shanty-town where non-Muslim Africans lived outside the city walls), but of course . . .

'It doesn't matter,' cried the Director's wife. 'There's Bill Tench. I can go with him.'

On Monday the Director wanted to know why Johnson had insulted his wife. He had refused her a lift in his car and talked about a date in the *Sabon Gari*; the first was no way to treat a lady in a hot country and the second, in view of the quarter's reputation, was an insult to her modesty. Johnson explained; the Director said 'All right laddie' and his wife hoped Johnson would 'soon learn how we do things here'. Mrs Director had many friends, whom she saw often. Johnson knew that his reputation round the club pool hung in the balance, and he took pains to be extremely correct with the new secretary when she eventually arrived.

Of course, the girl had to be offered some attention. A tour of the old city was an obvious start, so they climbed the minaret, explored the market, and ended up with a circuit of the ancient mud walls in the car. On the way back they met the vulture, sitting on the road as if waiting to be run over. Johnson explained that all vultures did that, but that they invariably flew out of the way at the last moment. With a contemptuous flap and a thump this one proved him wrong.

He stopped the car. The vulture had been thrown into the long grass beside the road where it was flopping about, obviously badly hurt.

'Oh, please kill it quickly!' cried the secretary, and hid her face in her hands.

Johnson disliked handling birds at any time – the touch of their feathers disgusted him. Of course, a hurt and bleeding bird was worse. A vulture was worst of all, because it was big and therefore probably difficult to kill, and because he always felt that under the black feathers the flesh of these carrion-eaters was rotting as they lived. But it was necessary to put on a brave show for the secretary. He decided to use the jack-handle. Resolutely, he grasped it and got out of the car.

The vulture lay with one wing awkwardly spread, rearing a heraldically angry head on a column of naked red neck. As Johnson approached it hopped and fell over. He chopped at it with the jack-handle and it squawked, cringing. He struck again and managed to draw the creature flapping messily on to himself. He shuddered, and threw a large stone, but still the black plumage struggled and flapped. He found an even bigger stone, mustered all his hatred, looked the vulture slap in the eye and dropped the boulder on its head. The stone rolled to one side, leaving the horribly flattened mask to rear slowly and jerkily on the column of neck, then droop and sway back to the ground. It must be dead. Johnson made a half-hearted attempt at making sure with the jack-handle, then went back to the car.

The secretary raised her face gratefully. They went for supper at the airport, and sat outside drinking liqueurs and watching an airliner that stared snootily over their heads being prepared for departure. Then Johnson took her home, making no attempt at a goodnight embrace – too soon yet – and drove off rather pleased with the showing he had made. As he passed the place where the vulture had been the headlights played over the long grass, but there was no movement. He returned his attention to the road and immediately stamped on the brake.

The car squawked to a stop in front of a dark bulk heaving on the tarmac. It was big, but indistinct: an injured cow or goat or something. Johnson groped for the jack-handle and grimly got out of the car. The creature heaved again and suddenly reared up towards him. He stepped back. It was an old woman, sitting up and rubbing her eyes. She scrambled to her feet and wrapped her cloth about her, apparently unhurt. Perhaps she had had a fall, or a fit, or perhaps she was mad. In gestures Johnson tried to tell her she shouldn't lie down in the road. She looked uncomprehending and whined. He led her firmly to the roadside, where she seemed very inclined to curl up as before. There wasn't much else he could do, so he got back in the car, tucked the jack-handle under the seat, and started off again.

The township was only a little way ahead, and before he reached the first bungalows he saw an African couple walking. They were young, and would surely speak English. He stopped and called them.

'There is an old woman lying in the road back there. I'm afraid someone will run over her,' said Johnson.

'You have run over her?' cried the young woman, and she began to yell for her companion, who had melted into the darkness.

Johnson got out of the car and tried to explain that he had not run over anyone, he only wanted the girl to tell . . .

But she was shouting too loudly to hear. 'You have killed ay wo-man!' she cried.

They both scrambled out of the road to avoid a passing car and as Johnson tried again to explain the girl struck at him with her handbag. A stream of cars was passing now, slowing down to avoid the gesticulating couple. The cinema was emptying. The girl was at last beginning to understand, but it didn't matter any more – either the old woman had gone away or these cars must have flattened her. But it was only when he glimpsed the shocked face of the Director's wife behind one of the windscreens that Johnson realized that the whole white community had seen him struggling at the roadside with a prostitute. They could hardly be blamed if they shared Mrs Director's doubts about the new officer now.

III Mr Gabriel

'Morning Sah,' said Mahmoud. 'Breakfass, he ready now.' That was to tell Johnson he was late.

'Just tea, Mahmoud.' Johnson had a hangover.

As he sipped and winced, a fat body got up from the far end of the veranda steps and bounced towards him, curling forward as it came, and pleating its stomach over the dirty trilby it was rolling up in its hands. It was Mr Gabriel, the auctioneer who disposed of government surplus.

'Good Morning Sah!' with a grin that was almost coy. He would not keep Mr Johnson long, but would you believe it? Since he had found Mr Johnson's house Mr Gabriel had been there two or three times, but had not dared approach. The fact was, his tongue was tied; yes, at the office and in public his tongue was tied. He came in and sat down, and agreed to a cup of tea.

Johnson sipped his tea and tried to make his eyes focus; Mr Gabriel emptied his cup in a single noisy draught and resumed his explanation. He could now see that he had been clumsy and given offence. Pardon his grossness, but he was not used to dealing with graduates. When he had asked Mr Johnson to dinner the other day he had asked a European lady too (the one who was now in unfortunate trouble for having been too friendly with Africans) and he had been clumsy and given offence; and in writing to Mr Johnson he had even addressed the letter wrongly and had not known how to set about putting it right. Mr Gabriel did not feel he was using his education properly in his present sphere, indeed, he wished to mix in better society and to improve himself. Also he felt terrible at taking all the commissions from the auctions; often he had brought some back to the office, but had not had courage enough. Surely it would be all right if after the auction he gave Mr Johnson a token of esteem?

Johnson repeated what he had said the last time: a 'token of esteem' was a bribe, and he would be suspected of corruption if the two of them met socially. So Mr Gabriel went out, backwards and still rolling his trilby. Then Johnson began to feel sorry that he had refused to eat with the man. The sentiment must have lingered, for the next time Mr Gabriel asked him out Johnson insisted on being the host himself.

He would not take Mr Gabriel to the guest house, for he remembered hearing a colleague say that he resented seeing Africans there – Christ! Europeans had a right to get away from the locals sometimes, didn't they? They would go to the airport hotel, where there were more strangers about and Johnson hoped he might not be recognized.

'Here I am!' Mr Gabriel bounced across the storm-drains to where Johnson's car came bumping over the earth roads of the southerners' settlement outside the Moslem city. He flagged the car down with a clean trilby, and as he introduced a young second wife – 'openly kept, unlike others' – Johnson admired his impeccable shirt.

As they drove to the airport, Mr Gabriel fumbled with some circumlocutory speech that suddenly spilled into blunt clarity:

'I don't know European ways of eating.'

Johnson made a vague depreciatory noise, and remembered how Africans ate *gari* paste with their fingers - very deftly and tidily, but . . .

'I hope you will advise me if I do anything . . . '

Johnson assured Mr Gabriel, as they passed through the haze of insects under the lamps, into the airport hotel lounge, that he would find everything quite simple and natural. Would he like a drink first?

'No, I should like to eat now.'

Good. They went into the dining-room.

Johnson thought he detected a smirk on the face of the Hausa waiter who advanced to meet them, and ignored him. He led Mr Gabriel to a table half-hidden behind a pillar. As the waiter bore down on them once more, Mr Gabriel again began to murmur his lack of confidence.

'I'll arrange for me to be served first, so you will see what to do,' said Johnson. The waiter received that instruction knowingly, and turned to Mr Gabriel:

'Soup or fruit-juice?'

Johnson leaned forward to help, but was forestalled.

'Both.'

And Mr Gabriel consumed them with noisy appreciation. 'I like to eat quite a lot,' he confided. But his bread-roll, held in a clenched fist when not being gnawed, became an embarrassment, so he guiltily hid it in his lap. Johnson advised him that he might lay it beside his plate, where it went and stayed, suffering hungry glances. Johnson looked at the menu; it was not very promising. Perhaps the airport hotel had been a mistake.

'What is this, please?' asked Mr Gabriel, pointing to an item on the list.

'I don't think spaghetti is a traditional African dish, is it?' replied Johnson, intending a warning.

'No, but I like to try new things.'

The waiter grinned in happy anticipation and set off to fetch two portions of spaghetti bolognese. Johnson disliked spaghetti, and the stuff the waiter brought was not a good example anyway. He forked up the trailing, vomity mess very

94

deliberately, hoping that Mr Gabriel was taking note of the method. Johnson made only one orange stain on the tablecloth and a couple of small spots on his shirt before he seduced the last yellow serpent into his mouth. Then he looked to see how his guest was doing.

Mr Gabriel sat with his hands folded on his belly before a clean plate. His shirt and the tablecloth were unsullied, and he belched encouragingly to the waiter, who looked quite put out as he cleared the plates and served the main course. Aggressively, he shoved the vegetable dish under Mr Gabriel's nose.

'I told you to serve me first,' hissed Johnson. The waiter loudly protested that it was not proper to serve the host before the guest, and Mr Gabriel looked miserable. He helped himself modestly to peas and chips – then took more chips. Clutching his knife and fork like drumsticks, he poked cautiously at his steak as if it might strike back. Johnson had run out of conversation. They had already discussed auctioneering exhaustively and Mr Gabriel did not want to talk about African traditional culture – 'Superstition, superstition! We are a Christian people.'

To break the silence Johnson threw out a name he had seen on countless hoardings:

'What do you think of the Action Group?'

Mr Gabriel ate with zest. He sent the waiter for water, for more bread; he refused ice cream (his teeth ached) and sipped coffee with the aplomb of a company director. As he ate, he talked. Johnson had never heard such a precise use of language in political exposition. For twenty minutes he was an entranced audience, penetrating the subterfuges of the western parties, regretting the benevolent wrong-headedness of the eastern leaders, weighing the chances of unity and the conflicting claims of tradition and innovation in the north, musing on the past splendour of the god-kings of Mr Gabriel's homeland and basking in the freedom from bias that was attributed to him.

An insect twanged at the other end of the room. Distracted for a moment, Johnson glanced up and caught the eye of the waiter, sidelong and ironic. He looked round the room and saw the other diners sitting very straight in their chairs; the only sound apart from Mr Gabriel's voice was the faint scraping of cutlery. Mr Gabriel had just finished waving his fork in the air and rolling his eyes as he rallied peasants; now he half-closed his eyes, stretched his short neck, and boomed down his nose in imitation of a neighbouring potentate. He leaned back in his chair and guffawed.

Chairs creaked unease and cutlery grated disapproval. Johnson was suddenly furious with this ugly fat man and his backyard politics. He stood up abruptly. It was time to go.

IV The Adventurer

Johnson had decided to have an adventure. He loaded cans of petrol and water into the car, waved goodbye to Mahmoud and smothered him in dust as he swept out of the compound. When he passed the club the long fair legs of the new secretary were already twinkling on the tennis court, but Johnson suppressed his regrets. There was a long weekend to mark some milestone or other on the road to Independence, and he was heading for the desert. He had read about a Frenchman who had gone with a camel caravan that fetched salt from a remote oasis, and he wanted to arrange to do the same – at Christmas, perhaps – and come back with a heroic sunburn and tales of sandstorms and mirages and nights under desert stars.

As he swerved round a double bend, a Fulani girl who had taken refuge by the roadside rocked her hips at him in a merry gesture. Another, surprised while peeing, scrambled to her feet, still balancing on her head the great calabash of milk she was taking to market. Johnson waved, and the girl grinned and waved back. Interesting people, the Fulani.

He drove north along a red scar of dirt road, with a great dust plume boiling behind him. Now the women he passed covered their faces or turned away. The men grinned bravely in the face of his dust and raised a fist in salute. Occasionally, he overtook lorries on their way from carrying groundnuts south, sprouting with the arms and legs of jammed passengers. He came up behind another, and bored into the red cloud through which he could just discern a cluster of black limbs swaying over double wheels. Then he blundered past under the driver's jutting elbow into clear air and the sight, surprisingly close, of a red-walled city built of mud. It was the last place in British territory.

He drank warm beer and ate a chicken, sitting on the midden that surrounded the crumbling walls. He added the bones of the chicken to the mound and drove on, across the unmarked frontier – there was a customs hut, but he overlooked it – into a belt of swamp where the spiky undergrowth might have inspired the Douanier Rousseau. When he abandoned the road to avoid floodwater, a termite nest hidden in the long grass left his bumper bent like the feelers of a beetle – the adventure was starting! It became dark, and the car thumped and bounced over even worse roads until it took a last jump and hissed along, apparently suspended six inches above the ground. He had reached the tarmac of the first French settlement.

In the square – for there was a square, with street lights – were African women wearing graceful sewn garments instead of breast-flattening mammy-cloths. There was even a small restaurant where, as he finished his meal, Johnson realized he had eaten better than he could have done anywhere in British territory. And on his way back to the unattended guest-house he heard dance music. It came from an open window. He looked inside and found a lanky African and a girl solemnly rotating in a padding, high-stepping waltz to the sound of a wind-up gramophone. Half a dozen other girls sat round the wall in splendidly patterned dresses. With grave courtesy the African relinquished his partner and drew another into his arms; he was evidently dancing with them all in turn. Johnson declined an invitation to join the rout and, having found his local colour, went satisfied to bed.

The next day he entered the desert – sheets of pebbles alternating with drifts of sand and enormous hard-baked expanses. The route was marked by cairns, occasional empty fuel drums, and wheelmarks. Blue-swathed Tuareg passed on camels; as they raised a fist in salute the blue cloth fell back and revealed a dagger strapped to each arm. There were dried-out carcases of beasts scattered along the way, and false impressions of water dancing at the horizon. The motor droned, rather thinly, perhaps. Suppose it broke down? Then how magnificently self-sufficient the Tuareg would seem!

He came round a stone-heap too fast and surprised a small caravan. The men leaped off the camels and clung to the headropes. The car slithered with locked wheels riding the dust and gently tapped the back of the last camel's legs. The beast immediately sat down and impressed the negative of its bony rump on the bonnet of the car. Then it teetered back to its feet and loped off, chased by its driver. The adventure was keeping up!

The car still worked and Johnson drove on across the dazzling surface. He swerved through another belt of dunes and sped over an enormous plain where the trail of tyremarks was scattered across half a mile. Then, on the horizon, and hard to see in the excessive light, there rose the finger of a mud-and-wattle minaret; he corrected his course and brought the car in a magnificent arc through the gateway of the mud-walled outpost.

There was a mud hotel with a shower consisting of a bucket

with holes in the bottom. Through the holes dripped the muddy water that a servant poured from a great jug while the bather stood underneath. A space under the central mud dome served as lounge, foyer and bar. There, Frenchmen wearing baggy black trousers with a filigree of braid down each leg and shirts with cutaway sides sat drinking wine and discussing the sterility of mules. Johnson had himself irrigated in the shower, then joined the conversation, contriving to be garrulous in tenseless French. He added to his opinion on the sterility of mules the praises of his car, that had braved collisions with camels, careered over dunes, sped across baked flatness and leapt all obstructions to bring him here.

'*Pourquoi*?' asked a thin Frenchman.

'*Pardon*?'

'*Pourquoi êtes-vous venu*?'

Johnson answered with a gesture that he felt to be very French and most expressive. It meant 'for the desert, the blue Tuareg, the enormous space, the unthinkably complex pattern of cracks in the miles of baked earth, the red city by the way, the heat that one defied to be hotter and yet it became hotter, the finger of the mosque rising on the horizon, the coming to a city out of the blank expanse and the glimpse of green palms that looked as an oasis should look.'

'*L'ennui, alors*,' said the Frenchman.

On Sunday Johnson went to counsult an '*ancien officier*' whom the hotelier recommended as knowing all about salt caravans and the possibility of joining one. The old hero sat at ease in a cool mud house, evidently enjoying retirement, though his *kepi* still hung behind the door. He was pink and plump, but with a formidable eye that must have been the terror of native levies. He, too, wore a shirt without sides and baggy black trousers with braid down the sides. He was in sandals, and exhibited powerful toes that somehow inspired Johnson with awe.

Naturally, he said, it was possible to go with a caravan to Bilma, if one wanted to do such a thing. But why? There was only sand – and a single tree, halfway there. It was *sans intérêt*.

Much better would be a tour in the mountains – *très jolie* – and particularly to be recommended if one had a little friend (he spoke judiciously, without a smile). No, it was not possible to hire camels, one must buy them and sell them again afterwards – and a saddle, of course. And one must take a gun.

Johnson loved it . . . 'Take a gun' . . . and his own camel saddle, with the inexplicable wooden cross that only Tuareg saddles bore mounted on the front – what a souvenir! Of course, he couldn't afford to do it, what with repaying his car loan, but it was something to have had the idea, and to have sat in solemn consultation with this tough old man with his mighty toes, his exotic costume and, no doubt, a native mistress in some domed and cushioned cell. It was surely an adventure just to meet him!

After lunch Johnson strolled in the market square. Robed men crouched in what little shade there was. The blue-black Tuareg watched like cats above the veils that covered their lower faces; their brown-black slaves tended screaming camels. There were indeed saddles for sale, and bowl-shaped blocks of brown crystalline salt, recommended against impotence. Johnson haggled for a lump, standing in the sun. The heat bore down out of a brass sky with a tangible weight; the square and its occupants could be seen only as a bleached monochrome through narrowed eyes. My God, it was hot!

He had to be back in the office for Wednesday, so he returned over the baked expanses, the sheets of pebbles and the dunes. The flood where he had detoured and hit the anthill had receded and the road ran, heavily rutted but intact, beside a shallow lake. Two naked young black women were in the water; they ran through a rainbow spatter of drops in half-feigned embarrassment, and the sun glinted on their wet skins as they laughed and waved behind him. You'd never see that in British West Africa. A little further on two ostriches sauntered across the road in front of the car. Then he met the hitch-hiker.

He was sitting, startlingly fair-haired and sunburnt like a fresh loaf, at the little travellers' shelter beside the last cluster of dwellings in French territory. His rucksack leaned against the wall, on top of which the few belongings he had unpacked were neatly stacked. He wore slacks instead of shorts, which gave him a peculiarly 'unofficial' air. He said he was waiting for a lorry – he didn't actually ask for a lift, but of course Johnson offered one.

With patent satisfaction he leaned back in the car as they bounced over the corrugations. He introduced himself as 'a painter and decorator to trade', and explained that he had set off down the A68 from Edinburgh six months ago to see something of the world. Crossing Europe he had stopped to work whenever money was low – oh, anything: picking grapes in France, kitchen work and painting houses with those funny brushes they used in Italy . . . North Africa had been interesting. He hadn't worked there, but that hadn't mattered much, because it was very cheap. He ate whatever the locals ate.

Oh no, the food hadn't been that bad. A bit monotonous, perhaps, but the Africans often wouldn't let him pay – he had never gone hungry. Ay, the couscous took a bit of getting used to, but there was often meat in it – a bit like a bad haggis (Johnson glanced sideways, uncertain if his leg was being pulled). He liked the bites of goat cooked on sticks best, and agreed that cassava paste was a bitty dull – but all right if you were hungry. The Africans made good soup, though; green things, mostly. He was lucky, he liked it spicy.

Johnson envied him for being fresh from Europe, where white women served in shops, pulled pints of beer, smiled, and constituted half the population. But his passenger didn't seem to recognize the importance of those things. He sat looking about him keenly and seemed delighted with everything he saw. It was nice to ride in a car, he said. He'd walked a three-hundred-mile stretch somewhere, after he'd lost all his belongings when a riverboat sunk. But mostly he'd travelled by lorry – oh, no, not the cab but in the back; the seat beside the driver cost extra!

He was permanently wide-eyed. Sometimes he quietly described what unreeled before him, sometimes he just sat looking, and absorbing. He observed the crops, and the differences from what he had seen further north. A group clustered round a boy with a drum delighted him. Oh, yes, they had drums in the desert; they had played them at a Tuareg wedding – there were camel races afterwards. Well, yes, he had done a bit of the journey on a camel – it was a spare one, and the drivers had seemed amused to have him with them. It was after that, when he was stinking of camel, that he got a lift in a French government truck; the officer who arranged it had seemed eager to get him out of his sector as quickly as possible. (He grinned at this, and Johnson wondered if he was really as naive as he seemed.)

'D'you know anyone in Kano?' asked Johnson, who had begun to be certain that the man would be deported as a vagrant.

– Oh yes, he had an old schoolfriend who was teaching carpentry at the Crafts School. It would be nice if he himself could get a job, but he doubted if that would be possible – not in a British colony.

Johnson agreed that it was very unlikely.

– He was looking forward to Kano, though – he'd heard a lot about it. He hoped to meet the Emir.

Johnson pulled a face at the road. He had only glimpsed the Emir at a distance, riding in processions under splendid umbrellas, or dispensing justice in his courtyard.

– And that old missionary lady who had bicycled up from the coast in 1910.

'1913,' corrected Johnson, a touch sharply. 'And what will you do after you've seen the sights of Kano?'

– He'd just go down to the coast and try to make his way along to Liberia – he thought that might be interesting.

'They'll probably put you on a ship when you get to Lagos,' said Johnson.

– Well, it would be better than walking back.

There was no answer to that.

Johnson offered dinner when they reached the city, but the hitch-hiker thought he ought to be getting along to his friends.

He would only come for a quick drink in the club. The place was almost empty, but Johnson introduced him as a fellow-countryman to a Scottish brandy-drinker who wiped his moustache and shook hands gravely, gazing into the hitch-hiker's eyes and uttering obscure Caledonian greetings. They chatted a little, then the hitch-hiker went to tidy himself before leaving. Johnson watched him cross the room; big, square-backed in his faded shirt, his crop of pale hair bleached paler at the top and the tan on his neck rusted with fresh sunburn.

'Your friend . . . ' said the Scot, gazing fixedly at the bottles that lined the back of the bar, 'bit of an adventurer, is he? Bloody adventurer?'

'Something like that,' said Johnson.

Yes. A bloody adventurer!

V Going Home

Johnson put down his glass; he was bored. The conversation at the bar was at the stage of swapping servant stories, each with a wide-eyed climax in pidgin English. Unable to think of a graceful excuse, he slid from his stool, rather aware of his legs, said a general goodnight and went out, upsetting only one chair and ignoring the surprised faces. He settled into his car with relief, backed away from the wall – the watchmen by the gate stirred as the headlights swept over them – then, suddenly unable to face the road home and the empty bungalow, launched himself in the opposite direction.

Five minutes later he came back past the club's whitewashed wall. There was in fact nowhere to go but home. His headlights played on the calves of an African girl sauntering ahead by the roadside. She looked back over her shoulder and his foot eased from the accelerator; as the car passed her she waved.

– And why not?

He stopped. A moment later someone scuffled at the door. She giggled, hiding her eyes; he opened the door and she got in, bringing with her a wave of cheap scent. Johnson moved off almost before the door was shut, and they drove towards his place in silence.

For once an African evening seemed to Johnson cool – even chilly – and the excitement in the pit of his stomach grew as they turned into the compound. Suppose Mahmoud were still there? But the house was in darkness. As he unlocked the door the watchman on the veranda looked up and murmured a greeting. Johnson remembered the groaning prayers that woke him in the night and did not dare look at the old Hausaman. In the bedroom he drew the curtains and switched on the light. The girl stood expectantly and his last courage drained away as he remembered someone telling him about a village where everyone had the pox and five out of six had both kinds. Why on earth had he brought her? He couldn't just say he'd changed his mind, could he? He groped for a way of saving face.

'I want to make picture of you,' he said '– without clothes.' He fetched his camera and menaced her with it. The girl seemed stupefied.

'You wish me naked?'

'Yes – like that,' and he showed her a photograph in *Lilliput*.

'Bloody European whore!'

'Yes. Now I make picture of you – very pretty.'

'No!' She was a prostitute, but too respectable to strip naked before a man '– unless you photo me in my knicker – ten shillings.'

Johnson was nonplussed. The girl wandered about as if she owned the place, picking up his things and examining them critically. She disappeared into the bathroom. Sulkily, he straightened the things she had interfered with and, when he heard her laughing, reluctantly went to see what she was doing. He found her sitting in the empty bath, her legs over the side, pretending she couldn't get out. She shook with giggling and her exposed thighs looked yellow and fat. Johnson told her to go. She demanded a ride back to the club; he took her, silenced her loud complainings in the roadway with a pound and drove back furious with himself.

Another car was in the compound and a lanky, pale-moustached figure was waiting on the veranda.

'Feel like a drink?' It was Cheetham, from the Public Works Department.

At Cheetham's they cleared the 'fridge of beer and finished off the whisky in the bottle. Then they sat glumly in the Public Works Department chairs while the ceiling fan thrashed away, its hub quivering in a vain attempt at penetrating the ceiling with its shaft. Finally, Cheetham suggested a trip to the *Sabon Gari* – he knew of a place that was quite fun.

Somehow Cheetham's car kept to the road and bumped safely over the ruts and conduits of the shanty-town outside the Moslem city. Johnson's head hit the windscreen as they lurched to a standstill before the dim light of a place labelled 'High Life Club'. Avoiding the eye of the Moslem policeman at the door, Johnson followed Cheetham into the mass of hot bodies swaying and shuffling on the cement floor to the ear-splitting din of a band.

A drink – from a bottle without a label, it seeemed. Johnson had another, then looked round for someone to dance with, and a girl was miraculously there – neat, in a pretty green dress. Cheetham was across the room by now, with a woman whose fuzzy hair had been ironed out straight. The band screeched and streamed with sweat; Johnson, who couldn't dance a step, danced superbly, exuberantly, frantically. He swung the girl off her feet, he tugged her and hugged her and shook her at arms' length; he tangled his feet, he recovered and reached for her, but the cement floor swung up and stopped, with a jerk, against his face.

Through a mist he approached a door; people were supporting him – fumbling in his pockets too. A taxi. Cheetham was there – no, he didn't want to go with him, he was all right. Ouf! The taxi was full of people, and hot. He was sick.

Johnson awoke in a low room, on a bed behind a curtain. It was day. An African lay beside him and when he sat up, dragging off the thin coverlet he found the simple nakedness of the girl he had danced with. Oh Lord!

The sequence of rousing her, sending her off on her bicycle for a taxi, and riding home in the shocking light of day passed in a daze – the headache hadn't really started. He paid the taxi extra because of the mess the night before. He had already paid the girl, who displayed a bruised cheek and broken lip and said she got them defending him, adding '– and you lay wid me proper – like mad!' – which surprised him.

He slouched into the house, and made for the bedroom.

'Mornin' Sah,' said Mahmoud. 'Breakfass, he ready now.'

Mahmoud did not like shopping in the 'canteens', or European-style shops. His English was hardly up to it, and he felt he was being cheated when he couldn't haggle. Besides, beer, paraffin and so on were awkward for a bicycle. So Johnson did the canteen shopping himself, leaving Mahmoud to go to market for vegetables, for the occasional live duck, which he brought home crucified on his bicycle's bumping carrier, or perhaps a hen, that swung and fluttered gaily on a string tied to the handlebars.

Thus it was Johnson who, a month or so later, waited for methylated spirits at the chemist's counter of United's. He hung about, reading about hairwash and deodorants, until the girl came back to tell him that that the methylated spirits was coming. She fished about behind the counter, and a moment later Johnson was surprised to hear her spitting. It seemed hardly the thing in the chemist's – still, this was Africa. The girl straightened up, wiping her mouth, and her face seemed familiar – but so many of them looked the same. She fetched the purple bottle, gave him change, then quickly ducked behind the counter again and he realized that she was retching.

Outside he pushed through the usual sticky press of small boys and cripples, avoiding the hands that offered to carry his bottles or receive his loose change. He now remembered why the girl had seemed familiar: she reminded him of the High Life Club – of the girl who had so merrily tweaked his woebegone cheek before pedalling off for a taxi.

But the resemblance was imperfect, he argued, as he drove away. And he couldn't possibly remember, through the barrier of a colossal hangover, a face seen in a drunken haze. The only image he could recall was of a girl gasping with excited laughter, and this one looked as miserable as the devil.

Still, he went as seldom as possible to the chemist's counter after that. And when next he had to replenish his supply of methylated spirits he saw that his guess had been correct; the girl's belly was swelling under the belt of her washed-out blue dress. She looked pale and unwell; she no longer ducked behind the counter to retch, but he fancied she looked at him reproachfully. He felt quite nervous when, leaving some films to be developed, he had to give his name and address. But nothing happened. Of course not.

Buying soap he surreptitiously studied the weary eyes, the nose that was flat yet delicate, with a tip that moved slightly as she spoke, and the high cheekbones – that was what was so disturbing; those high cheeks. He tried to visualize the lips that now hung sulkily between them lifted and parted in laughter. He simply couldn't be sure – but he couldn't believe . . . Wouldn't she have taken precautions? Of course, Africans didn't go in for that sort of thing, but she did work in the chemist's and daily dispensed little packets to gruff white men and little boxes to sour white women. But in any case it was impossible. It was stupid to think about it.

At last the date of his leave came through. Europe was suddenly a few days and a short ride along the dusty airport road away. The idea of anything physically connected with him being left in Africa was monstrous. He put it out of his mind. No doubt the bulge behind the chemist's counter continued to grow, but he forgot about it in the excitement of getting tickets, and the confusion of selling his car and household goods and packing the few belongings he would take with him.

The night before he was due to leave he stood outside concentrating on his last African evening. He tried to identify the constellations; there was the plough, of course, but the mango trees always hid the southern cross. The stars he could see would still be with him tomorrow night, over the desert; the next morning he would be in the streets of Rome. Now he could hear the frogs starting their croaking in the club pool a couple of miles down the road and, faintly, the sound of the flannel-dance gramophone. From further off came the inevitable pulse of a drum; didn't they ever tire of it? Two notes: de-boom, then a little tune of four notes: de-boomity boom de-boom, over and over again.

He listened intently. There was something new: the sound of a pipe. It seemed to come from the new Syrian house across the way – a fine affair of white columns and balconies and fretted balustrades, but always empty. And there it was again – unmistakably a flute. Like clear running water the sounds chased each other, slipping into quarter-tones, lingering, then skipping away again, silvery like the moonlight on the stirring mango leaves.

He went across. The playing stopped, leaving an emptiness through which he crunched up the new laterite path. A black shape stirred in the shade of the ostentatious steps: the night-watchman.

'*Sanu*,' said Johnson – at least he knew that much Hausa.

'*Sanu*, *sanu*, and long life, white man.'

'Where is your flute?' Embarrassed at his own pantomime, Johnson whistled over his fingers.

The watchman laughed and drew a slip of silver out of his rags. He began to play. Nearly naked, very black and indistinct,

with a tuft of beard that showed when he turned to spit, he crouched and played liquid music on his flute. Shoulders and head intent, a poor man consoled himself for a hard life by drawing a sequence of sounds from the night.

'May I see your flute?'

'*Aie*,' and he offered the slender, silvery instrument. Johnson took it and was astonished by its weight. It was made from a length of gas piping.

'*Sai gobe*,' he said.

'*Sai gobe*. Till tomorrow; sleep well, white man.'

The day came. The morning refused to pass. The new secretary – who was not so new by now – gave him lunch. Then it was time. She got into the Fiat *topolino* of which she was so proud and when she leaned across to unlock the passenger's door Johnson peeped into her low-cut frock and felt a moment's regret for Africa. Then they were off, in good time because they had to cross the centre of town.

'Just a minute,' said Johnson, as they bumped into the street where the big canteens were. 'I just want to slip into United's.'

He went into the cool of the canteen, incongruous in sports jacket and flannels among the shirts and shorts. She stood behind her chemist's counter, quite enormous. He felt sure this bloated creature wasn't the girl from the High Life, but . . . she looked coldly at him. Was it because he regularly brought methylated spirts that he thought he detected recognition in her mournful gaze? He felt for his wallet; he had been paid quite a lot. Then he walked quickly to the liquor counter and bought a magnum of champagne.

Half of it spurted through the open roof when he uncorked the bottle in the jolting car. He and the secretary drank the rest between them, straight from the bottle, and Johnson's incisors clinked convivially on her rather endearing buck teeth as she kissed him in a final moment of unwonted warmth.

'Reason for leaving Nigeria,' said the emigration form.

'Boredom,' he scrawled and walked, not very steadily, to the aeroplane.

The Major Steps Out

Major Inscape considered the hypothesis that women were no longer attractive to him. To test it he eyed the girl next to him in the supermarket queue. Her head reached to his chest, which ought to make him feel protective; she had delicate bones and, as she looked down at her basket to check that she had everything necessary for supper for two, her heavy eyelids took on a touching sweetness. But Major Inscape was unmoved.

Conscientiously furthering his experiment he swayed forward slightly and looked down the girl's open blouse. Dully he noted the bifurcated roundness that thrust toward the two dark accents that showed on the outside of the cheesecloth. The girl turned and looked at Major Inscape suspiciously; the Major smiled at her as he swayed back, and she smiled too. No doubt she had recognized that he was no longer interested in women.

Major Inscape weighed the economical fullness of a pair of jeans in the next queue with complete indifference. Mentally he peeled off the tight clothes and held a compact body to his own lean frame; it engendered only a sense of chill. At a nudge from the basket behind he moved on to the checkout and his eyes ski'd down the vertiginous slopes that swept from the chin of the girl at the till into the dark valley of her *décolletage*, and he was bored.

From then on it was downhill all the way. He averted his gaze from the bodies that deployed muscle and limb to manoeuvre wilful trolleys through the racks of groceries. The poster of a near-naked girl over the suntan section was less interesting than the diagram of beef cuts over the butcher's counter. He paid, gratefully accepting the smile with which the Queen of the Slopes acknowledged his offer of the right money. She was clearly a nice person – like all the rest of these women and girls: kind sisters, loving mothers; much nicer than men. And much nicer than they had seemed to be when they were the objects of his desire.

It was the same with Barbara. He'd first noticed it with her, of course. Dear girl; pleasant to talk to – well, would be, if they hadn't said everything in thirty years of marriage; good gardener . . . he had a lot to be thankful for, though there was something in what old Carstairs used to say when he held forth in the mess before lunch:

'Remember, my boy, that the trouble with wives is that before you know where you are they've become one of the family. Instead of abetting your debonair extravagance they join up with the bank manager. What's more, sexual relations with 'em become a form of incest!'

It was true that over the past few years Major Inscape's attitude to his wife had become increasingly fraternal. Now, arrived at his gate, he admired the tidying that Barbara had done in the herbaceous border, and was cheered to see her through the window, reading the paper, no doubt with a glass of sherry beside her. The prospect of a drink and a ritual exchange of banalities was comfortable. It was that damned supermarket that had put him in the dumps – no place for a chap, really, even if the sherry was cheaper.

But his disturbing state of mind recurred the next morning on the station platform. Around him the suburban typists and secretaries stood like well-groomed yearlings on their slim hocks. They were simply not as interesting as the horses would have been, even when they moved nervously from hoof to hoof and raised their pretty muzzles enquiringly towards the tunnel. Horses would have had finer drawn heads, and glossy masses instead of these pert bulges. Major Inscape studied the cast-iron tracery of the station canopy instead.

The final confirmation of his condition was given by a graceful mulatto emerging leggily from a Cadillac as he came up the steps from the Underground. He found he simply didn't care, and by the time he reached his room in the Ministry he was quite cheerful. Ater all, a chap couldn't very well regret a desire he no longer possessed.

He acknowledged Miss Yarborough's gargled greeting, but for some reason her crisp white blouse, blushing at the shoulders and lacy at the front, depressed him again. Pity they had taken out the old coal fires. Poking them and setting fire to the carpet – which in his grade reached to the fender but not to the wall – used to cheer him up.

As it was, he perked up at the sight of a full in-tray. There was that business about whether a citizen of one of the oil states should be sent back home, where he claimed he would have his hands cut off. An interesting and complex question, bearing in mind the British government's desire for cordial relations with the régime and the local British representative's doubts about the reliability of the assurances that had been given. Major Inscape tucked into the papers with relish, but after a few minutes he leaned back in his chair and stared out of the window. It was all so petty. The chap wasn't to have his hands cut off at all; only to be castrated.

Major Inscape's window was on the Embankment side of the annexe, looking out on the Thames. Today the river was murky grey; an enormous volume of rather dirty water, heaped up in slow, thick-skinned waves that occasionally broke in yellowish foam. There were not so many barges now. A few years ago there would have been a succession of tugs bullying through the sullen water, but the river was running down like everything else – like the docks, the railways and British Leyland – like Major Inscape's libido.

And that had once blazed as furiously as any furnace in the Workshop of the World. The Major remembered the aching longing that had even put him off his food – and he had always been omnivorously hungry. It had been bad enough during national service, when his fluke promotion – the result of a flair for languages – had made him the baby of the mess and terribly self-conscious. It had been the general view that he was too young for most off-duty expeditions, and he had been left to hunger quietly.

At university he had been a conscientious scholarship man, grubbing for a first (which he hadn't got) and it had been just as bad. There had been pub crawls and drinking parties, but they were all-male affairs. He had once gone to a tea party in a women's college and had spent a very painful hour because he was too shy to ask the way to the lavatory. It wasn't like that nowadays. When he had visited his daughter at her college he had stood and gaped in admiration. There were chaps in the bath calling for the soap and girls running down the corridor in their nighties fetching it for them. O brave new world!

God, the time he must have wasted staring at the red – or were they green? – curtains of his room, thinking about girls. When he revisited the college he couldn't remember which room had been his, but the image of that book-strewn table with the wrought-iron lamp and that curtain (it had been green, he was certain), on to which he had projected so many lubricious fantasies, would always encumber some attic of his mind.

Behind the green curtain, and behind the fretted stone mullions, lay the dark pool of the quad, with islands of yellow light under the lamps and the hall sailing out into the lawn like a galleon. Beyond the gatehouse lay the town, and a world of which half the population was female. There were the nurses from the infirmary and the girls from the marmalade factory, so liltingly praised by Jenkins, the Welsh debauchee. And there were whole colleges full of female undergraduates.

He saw them when he went to the library: the wilting blonde who was towed out to coffee by a different pair of cavalry twills each morning; the dazzler who had looked up at him appealingly from the tangled chain of her bicycle – he had smiled and hurried on, perfectly willing to help but reluctant to seem eager, though he had just sat through an entire lecture entranced by her hair. Instead of deftly fixing the chain and proposing coffee in the Cadena, or perhaps an afternoon on the river, he had gone back to stare out of the window and, after dinner, to dream before his curtain.

That could well have been the night when there had come the knock at his door. He had supposed it was someone wanting to borrow butter, but instead of big Harry from the room opposite, or the organ scholar from one flight down, there stood this girl. A girl, come to his door! He recognized her as one of the college reps of the United Nations Society, or something of the sort, of which he was secretary. Occasionally, he had accidentally caught her eye at meetings and thought she looked less inaccessible than some of the others in her simple outfit of blue skirt – perhaps her old school skirt – black sweater and short duffel. Now, a neat figure on his threshold, she gave a quick, nervous smile and started to speak, but her voice was husky and she had to clear her throat and lick her lips before starting again. Was there a meeting of the Society this evening, she asked.

He couldn't remember. How stupid – he was the secretary, after all! He scrabbled among the papers on his desk, then turned with a light laugh to the mantelpiece, from which he dislodged his clock into the fender. Still no luck, but hold on! There'd be a notice in the lodge, of course. He'd run down and see – no, honestly, it wouldn't take a second.

He clattered down the stairs and ran to the lodge, but there was no notice because he hadn't pinned one up. He ran to Carter's room and Carter was very hesitant but thought he probably didn't know either. As he ran back across the quad he hardly believed she would still be there – weren't girls supposed to be out of men's rooms by this time? At the top of three flights of stairs he was breathless.

No, he didn't think there was a meeting, he gasped.

And she went.

Major Inscape was aghast at his youthful blindness. Only now did he see the incident clearly and realize why she had come, dry-lipped and nervous, to his room. She could easily have found out about the meeting without doing that. She had a card with the programme, as college rep she should have posted a notice in her own lodge, and in any case there must have been girls in her college who could have told her. Any fool could see she knew there was no meeting. She must have gone away hating him for his stupidity.

And it had always been like that, even after he had gone back for his second stint in the army. He remembered the CO's daughter at Bielefeldt and kicked the leg of his desk in shame.

Barbara had come along, of course, but she didn't really count, even though he had fathered two children on her. She had made most of the running at first, and eventually it had seemed sort of accepted that they should get married. They had been as happy as most couples. They never quarrelled. She had been an excellent wife, in a plain-cooking sort of way. Uncomplicatedly willing, sexually, she had brought an energetic and rangy body to their couplings. Major Inscape regretted none of all that. But the earlier years of quite unnecessary and unwilling monasticism, they struck him as an irreparable loss.

If he had only taken that girl to the cinema that night, or to the Playhouse! She was quite nice to look at, but not dauntingly beautiful. She would probably have turned out rather dull, but could hardly have been duller than the fellows he went around with. For some reason she had been drawn to him; her shy, dry lips declared it, and her modest anatomy might eventually have yielded him limited but cathartic privileges. At least, her sane womanhood might have straightened him out a little. But he had turned her away.

Thinking of the golden hours and silly joys that were lost, Major Inscape kicked the leg of his desk again, so that he did not hear Miss Yarborough's knock as she came bringing files and a discreet breath of perfume into the room. Suddenly she was before him, turning over the papers in his tray like a young horse at its fodder. With cold deliberation and a complete absence of enthusiasm Major Inscape reached out and seized a generous segment of her left butttock.

'Haha-a-ah!' he cried, as obbligato.

From the bubbly texture under his fingers he deduced that Miss Yarborough wore lace about her loins; a great gilder of lilies, Miss Yarborough. But now she arched her back and curvetted away with a snort of astonished laughter.

'Major Inscape!' she whinnied.

Major Inscape was surprised to find his heart thumping. He had embarked on a motiveless act and suddenly desire was draining the strength from his limbs. Deeply embarrassed, he returned to his papers, then forced himself to look up at Miss Yarborough over his spectacles. He was in time to receive a coy backward look as, tossing her yellow mane, she

116

trotted out of the room.

When he had calmed down he found that the rediscovery of his interest in women did not cheer him at all. It was quite unimportant. Nothing that happened now could make up for what had not happened in the past. That supreme callowness of so many years ago had sealed his fate in a way. Anyone who could be as stupid as that was never going to be much good. He had said no to life on the threshold of his study thirty years ago, and nothing could make up for it.

He could not be bothered with Mohammed Daud's application to remain in the United Kingdom.

'Recommend expedite deportation', he wrote. The fellow would probably be better off without his balls. Pushing back his chair, he got up and walked over to the window. The Thames was drearier than ever, and quite empty of traffic. Peering down he could see the junior minister getting out of a car at the entrance below; even from this angle he looked very self-important. Major Inscape had to climb on to the bench below the sill to open the casement. A gust of wind brought the flat tang of the estuary up the river as he stepped out. As he fell he thought of the old joke about it being 'all right so far' and smiled.

Summer Pudding

Bert lay in the shade of the upturned tumbril. Or rather, he reclined. Leaning on one elbow, his waistcoated paunch comfortably settled, with one leg drawn sideways and the other curled along the ground, he contemplated the world. The pose left his guts nicely cradled and his head upright, a swivelling turret from which he could keep watch and discharge bursts of speech through the flat embrasure of mouth.

The stackyard was a pleasant spot. Great trees bowed graciously from the margin, extending arms hugely clothed in leaves. Their hollow volumes were peopled with birds; you could hear them stirring – but very gently, in this heat. Between Bert's nest under the old cart, and mine beside the burnished spikes of the tractor wheel, was a patch of sunlight almost too brilliant to look upon. I looked instead into my sandwich tin, chose a slab of bread and cheese and fed it into my mouth with the end of a spring onion; harvesting was hungry work.

Bert, too, without disturbing the main elements of his posture, had drawn his army surplus haversack to him and fetched out his tin and flask. Now he sipped tea with his shovel mouth, and pronounced on his fellow-workers – not Billy and Dick who worked with us, but the house servants, mainly.

'Take that chauffeur. Doctor told his wife after the last time that she warn't to have any more family, but I saw her this morning . . .' he sucked in his breath through the corner of his mouth '. . . he'd been there again, y'see!'

I sighed deprecation and Bert prepared to drink more tea. The birds stirred.

'Whussat?' Bert traversed his head to attend to a mild

clanking sound. I looked up and saw a gaunt bicycle come wobbling through the entrance to the stackyard. With a scuffle of strap-and-button shoes and a scissoring of skinny legs in milk-tea stockings the rider sprang off. Bert did not look round.

'Wuh!' It was a grunt of enquiry, a gruff challenge that a lazy dog might have issued in lieu of a bark as it wearily dragged itself up to face someone it knew well. But Bert continued to recline, and to face away from his wife as she wheeled her tall bicycle to a tree and leant it there.

'There you are, then, Bert!' Her voice wobbled and wavered over most of an octave, very like the way her bicycle wobbled and trailed about the road. I had met her that morning as I rode to work. She had come over the top of Hoxton hill, her head waving from side to side behind her towering handlebars; elbows out, knees cranking, drifting and staggering about as if there were a high wind. She waved gaily as she passed:

'Hello! I'm late for work today, y'see!'

I believe she did some cleaning up at the House.

Now she carrolled: 'I've brought you a nice hot pudden, Bert.' Her eyes were bright with scheming pleasure behind her round glasses as she brought her basket across and set it down beside the square-faced reclining buddha. 'I thought I might have a bite out here with you.'

'Wuh!' scolded Bert. He eyed the basket, nobly covered with a faceted white cloth. His wife folded her awkward legs like some lanky animal of the plains and settled, with a tucking under of petticoats, to the ground. Then she smiled round at the stackyard and at me, and flashed her glasses up at the trees where the birds fluttered their irritation at this breach of their peace.

'There!' she said, and turned her attention to the basket. 'Tha's a beef pudden, Bert.' She removed the cloth and folded it carefully. Then she fetched out a bundle loosely tied in another cloth – a coloured teacloth, this time – which she deftly undid. Last came the pudding-cloth itself, tight round the top of the basin, and a vexatious delay while the string was plucked undone – I stuffed another slab of bread and cheese into my mouth and had difficulty in returning the conspiratorial smile that was tossed my way. The pudding-cloth was finally removed; greaseproof paper was peeled away, and steam softly rose.

'Tha's got an onion in, Bert.' She set out two plates.

Bert looked away, his mouth set in a straight pouch with tucked-in corners. 'I en't a lover of hot food out,' he said. When he spoke his mouth opened squarely, like a letterbox, and his lower lip shovelled the words out.

'A beef pudden with an onion innut, Bert,' said his wife. 'I know you'll enjoy that.' She fetched a table knife out of her basket and plunged it into the plump, pale belly of crust. More steam. From the other side of the patch of sunlight I breathed the richness of slowly cooked meat; of gravy's unhurried gestation in a womb of crust that gently partook of the transformation within its walls. I pitied the uninstructed Mediterranean, feeding on pasta smeared with a perfunctory sauce, ignorant of the close, considered secrets of a suet pudding. Replete on bread and cheese, I still found moisture gathering in my mouth as Bert's wife spooned, and I wondered if the decline of Rome could be traced to the arrival of the caravan that brought the recipe for noodles along the silk road and displaced the invention of the pudding to the boundaries of Europe.

To avoid intruding I leaned back on the tussocks by the tractor wheel and closed my eyes. I enjoyed the comfort of the soft, dry grass, the sound of the birds moving in the green caverns of the great trees, the distant rocketing of a pheasant and the smell – lovely to anyone who worked in a harvest field of those days – of ripe corn mingled with a faint reek of the paraffin the tractors ran on. And now, of course, a rumour of the higher arts; the drifting smell of Bert's wife's pudding.

I looked across at them. Mrs Bert had charged her husband's plate heavily, her own hardly at all. Bert casually picked up the fork she had laid ready and, still leaning on one elbow, stabbed at his plate. He conveyed the food to his coal scuttle mouth and snapped at it.

'Isut all right Bert?' asked his wife.

Bert grunted. 'I en't a lover of hot food out,' he growled, and snapped up another forkful.

'Well Bert, I thought you'd be tired of sandwiches and enjoy a change. Tha's hard work in the harvest I know –' she turned to me '– en't it, Will? Don't you find it hard work?'

I said yes, I did.

'But I expect you enjoy it, don't you? That'll be a change for you. Tha's nice to have a change sometimes.'

I agreed, and exchanged smiles with her, then lay back again. The scraping of Bert's fork mingled with the confidential rustling of a beetle near my ear and the cooing of woodpigeons in the trees. After a while the fork clattered on the plate. I looked and saw Bert licking his fingers and shoving his plate away.

'There, tha's all I want.'

'Well there,' said his wife, gathering the two plates and tossing the morsel of crust that Bert had left to where a sparrow bobbed hopefully. 'I thought you might have enjoyed that.'

Bert grunted. 'You know I en't right a lover of hot food out,' he said.

We rested in silence for a few minutes.

'Well, I shall have to be getting on,' said his wife, loosening her bundled legs. She delayed to scrabble after some periwinkles – 'Tha's pretty' – and dropped them into her basket beside the carefully arranged basin and plates. Then she covered everything with crisp white decency and staggered to her feet. She hung her basket on the handlebars of her tall bicycle, warbled a farewell, put a foot on a pedal and gathered the other through the deep curved gap in the ladies' frame. Bits of fern caught in the spokes buzzed in the skirt-guard of fanned cords that extended round the rear mudguard. As she wobbled through the stackyard gate she met Billy and Dick, returning from dinner in the village.

'Afternoon Mr Wells, afternoon Mr Glimmer!'

'Here y'be then, Mrs Boggis, here y'be.'

As the clanking of her bicycle faded Billy Wells sniffed the air: 'Wuh Bert, I do believe your missus has been bringing you hot vittles.'

'Wuh!' said Bert.

'Now then Bert,' said Dicky Glimmer, 'you'll be knocking hell out o'them poor sheaves after that.'

'Wuh!' said Bert. 'That was her idea. I en't a lover of hot food out,' and belching gently he got to his feet.

After a decent pause Billy stretched his scrawny neck and addressed no one in particular: 'Well, le's be having you. Them sheaves are waiting and the one we're looking for is out there somewhere.' I knew that the one we were looking for was the last sheaf of the day.

Old Linge emerged from behind the cart, where he had lain forgotten, and folded his ancient leather hand round the shaft of a pitchfork. I, proud at knowing how, set the throttle of the tractor, checked that it was out of gear and the clutch-brake was down, turned the pointer on the tank to 'petrol' and cranked. We clambered aboard, me behind the wheel and old Linge on the wagon, and I steered after the others as they processed into the blazing yellow sunlight. Out in the middle of the field Aubrey already had the tractor of the binder running, making the air shimmer with its exhaust.

'We ought to clear this up by five o'clock,' said Billy. 'There'll be some rabbits in there, I reckon.'

'There's one in there 'cos I see it come out,' guffawed Dick. It was an old joke based on an utterance from Old Linge two days before.

'Ah,' retorted Old Linge. 'So there is, more 'n one, I'm sure.'

Out in the field Aubrey wallowed and bounced his broad backside in the sprung seat of his tractor as it lurched over the uneven ground. The binder chattered after, sails turning, bending the corn on to the shivering blades of the cutter. Barley, poppies and rare cornflowers fell. So did harvest mice if they hadn't fled in time. All were carried up the slatted canvas and across the bridge over the great central wheel, where a curved needle swooped to stab twine round each bundle and declare a sheaf.

The binder circled the standing corn, feeding on its edge and dropping sheaves across the stubble. Bert and Arthur worked along the rows, piling sheaves into stooks with a flick that looked effortless until you tried to do the same. Bert had shed his hat and his bald head shone. Billy Wells, stripped to his vest, exposed indecently white skin beyond his chestnut elbows. Squinting into the sun and sneering with effort, he pitched sheaves up to Old Linge, who laid them in the wagon cunningly, the outside ones pinned fast by those he trod into the middle. That way the mounting load stayed firm as the cart jolted and swayed.

The continent of golden barley slowly diminished. It had been dwindling all day; imperceptibly at first, and for a long time retaining the broad square shape of the field. Then, as it grew smaller, it had become elongated, until now only a long tapering island remained. We stopped, and wandered to the shade for 'fourses' – the House had sent out a small keg of beer that was hung from a convenient branch. Then Billy Wells led us out again, and the island grew smaller still.

When it was only a hundred yards long and a few paces wide, Bert and Arthur left their stooks and stood waiting. Billy Wells stopped pitching sheaves and Old Linge clambered deliberately down from the wagon. Dicky Glimmer, his shirt open to the waist, and red as a beetroot from his tuft of hair down to the pit of his skinny belly, came from the stackyard with Tom the stacker. Everyone gathered expectantly round the last ranks of corn.

Aubrey floundered voluptuously on his sprung seat, leaning out and looking back as he drove the cutter into the cliff of stalks. Surely the dangling ears were stirred by something other than the eddies of superheated air?

'There's one in there 'cos I see it come out,' bawled Aubrey for the hundredth time.

At that moment a rabbit did break out. Dick ran too soon and it doubled back into the corn. From behind Dick another flash of grey-brown scuttled. Dick ran a few steps, but this time he was too late. He turned back, shaking his head, then slapped his thigh in vexation at seeing yet another white tail sneaking into the bracken at the field's edge. Aubrey laughed as he swung the tractor out, then in again for another cut on the far side. His voice sounded above the roar and chatter of the machinery as he bounced about in front of the whirling sails:

'There's one in there . . .'

Billy Wells suddenly flung himself down on his face, clutching a convulsion beneath him. He chuckled into the stubble, baring his upper teeth as he did when he swung the sheaves over his head. Now he brought the rabbit up, quickly stretched its neck and laid it, still twitching, by his jacket. A keen nose bent, sniffed it, and passed on. Harry Lark the keeper had come with his dog and gun.

'Get you over the other side, Harry, and watch what you're a-doing,' said Old Linge. Harry made a grim face but did as he was told. Guns and chasing rabbits don't mix. He stationed himself by the point of the wedge of corn, his dog beside him, its backside dropped but not quite touching the ground, grinning, and dismissing with a jerk and return of its head my offer to distract it with a pat.

From the boundary of the field came a flutter of pale linen. Two women, one buxom and majestic, the other teetering on thin bare legs, embarked on the stubble, with a smaller blue dress cavorting and drifting behind. It was the housekeeper and one of the maids, with young Nancy.

'Come on, Mrs Backus,' shouted Billy. 'We need some runners. Le's see you hitch up your skirts!' Mrs Backus laughed, and jostled her bulk in a couple of playful steps. 'I may yet,' she called back.

For the final cut we all gathered in close. The tractor roared and the binder flailed through a haze of dust. Rabbits ran, and we ran after them. Dick's long body leaned back as he pelted on short bow legs and white teeth flashed in his turkey-red face.

'Yip-yip-yip-yip-yip!' he shouted.

The rabbit darted and dodged, bouncing in the stubble that caught on its belly and hindered its legs. Then it slowed, head and ears laid back, and gave a thin scream of despair just before Dick pounced and rose, his face redder than ever, to still the leaping at the end of his arm with a quick jerk. No sooner had he dropped the rabbit than he was off again, to sprawl full length with another struggling in his stretched grasp. Billy Wells scurried in the other direction, half double, arms drooping like a gorilla's, anticipating the rabbit's twists and turns, then

125

swooping on it. Even Old Linge managed to block one with his pitchfork and grab it before it could run on.

Bert held to his strategic position between the end of the corn and the nearest boundary. Suddenly he made a little sideways shuffle and trapped a rabbit between his boots. Expending the minimum of effort, he dodged to and fro over the stubble and met the terrified animals as they fled from the clamour behind. He had another with a kick and a pounce, and sank majestically to pin down a third.

I ran after rabbits too, half afraid of catching one. Then as I gained on a bobbing scut, I found myself 'yip-yip-yipping' just like Dick. When the rabbit slowed and laid its head back on its desperately bouncing shoulders I had it, and held it up in triumph by the hind legs. It arched its back and I chopped hopefully at its nape. At first I could hardly believe that the mechanically convulsing body was so easily dead, then I proudly carried it to the field's edge, with blood gathering on the end of its nose.

'Gi'e us it,' said Bert. He stood by a little row of gutted rabbits. There was a rich, gamey smell of blood as he whipped his knife, smeared and stuck with downy filaments, the length of the white-furred belly. Inside all was neatness and bright pastel colours and the packed innards gleamed with a light wetness. With two fingers Bert drew out the guts and dropped them into the dusty mess at his feet. 'There y'are,' and he handed the stained corpse back to me.

Out in the field there was a last commotion. Young Nancy, her skirt tucked up in her knickers, was pelting after a rabbit, converging with Dick. He gallantly slackened his pace and she bent, grabbing and clutching as she ran, but the rabbit bounced over her hands and vanished into the bracken. Nancy returned proudly to where the women were coming off the field. That was the last of it.

'Wuh, come on!' Bert scolded me. 'We've got the rest to fetch in yet. Set your rabbit along o'mine under the cart. That oon't take no harm.'

I carried the rabbit across and bent under the old tumbril. The grass in its shade was still green, and Bert's bag lay with his rabbits in the cool, and his hat alongside with folded dockleaves laid over it. Inquisitive, I lifted the leaves. In the upturned crown of the hat was a posy of mixed flowers. There were poppies, of course, and he had hunted down some cornflowers and wild marigolds and musk mallows, toadflax and other things I couldn't put a name to. He must have found them for her at 'fourses' time, when we were all gulping the Colonel's beer.

The shovel mouth snapped: 'Come on, Bor! The sheaf we're looking for is still out there somewhere!'

Feet of Clay

Crayon scraped paper. Occasionally there was a deep intake of breath or a heavy sigh; less frequently, the snap of a breaking stick of charcoal or the light, musical clatter of a dropped pencil followed by the scramble of its recovery. From behind a semicircle of easels, or astride the short benches known as 'donkeys', twelve young people glared in concentration at a thirteenth, who lay silent and immobile. She was Brenda, their model, the focus of their attention and the occasion of all the petty movements of their industry. In contrast to the colourful and often bizarre costume of the others, Brenda was naked.

There was a fourteenth person in the room. He was clothed in a considered combination of deep green jacket, rust shirt and buff moleskin trousers. He passed from easel to easel, studying the drawings and darting keen, verificatory glances at the model. After each appraisal Maurice – that was his name – would comment in a low voice that seemed uncomfortable at striking out alone across the hushed studio. At certain points the voice dropped to a whisper:

'. . . And this passage here, from the top of the arm across to the – ah – (hushed and breathless) – *breast* . . . '

At the end of each visitation Maurice, with a doubtful sideways glance to see that he had been understood, and another quick look back at the model, to check that she was still present and in good order, moved on, leaving a student dabbing dejectedly at the flat paper on which he was trying to conjure the emphatically three-dimensional form of Brenda's body.

Brenda, ex-electronic assembly worker, ex-gogo dancer, ex-wife to a merchant seaman and current occasional bedfellow to Seamus, a heavy-breathing Scot who had just broken his charcoal on her navel, flexed a stiffening knee with an apologetic smile. Maurice waited with delicately manifested patience until she was settled, and turned to yet another drawing board.

'That's coming along quite well, Graham. Watch the proportion – remember to stand back from it occasionally,' and he moved on to Graham's neighbour. 'Now, Fiona.'

Fiona tossed back her loosely tied fair hair and smiled one of those astringent smiles in which the corners of the mouth are drawn down instead of up, as she made room for him at her easel.

Her movement brought her nearer to Graham, and he breathed her faint, distinctive perfume with gentle excitement. He had contrived to place his easel next to hers. Now he stepped back, combining obedience to Maurice's instruction with a prospect of Fiona's graceful hand-on-hip stance, and at the same time offering her a chance to admire his drawing. He thought it rather good. Her own work was neat and competent but even he, who wanted to find only perfection in her, had to admit that it was not very remarkable.

But Fiona was absorbed in what Maurice was saying, and Graham could only marvel at the way her dress seemed exactly right. He did not dream how much it had cost, but Brenda did, and resented the idea.

'When I see her come drifting into the studio all done out to kill, and me standing there starkers I could *spit!*' she had told Seamus, spraying indignant crumbs all over the sandwich bar.

Graham attributed all the grace of Fiona's clothes to the refinement of the structure beneath them. Squinting sideways at her, he applied the residue of anatomy lectures to the points of suspension and the nuanced fall of her bodice and skirt. He constructed a shoulder girdle of delicate wings and struts, poised over a symphony of ribs. He calculated the projection and weight – no, weightlessness – of the entities that nudged the crisp cotton. He placed the curve of her iliac crest and, as opportunity and her posture offered, admired the modest – but perfect – swell of her left great trochanter. He longed to discern the forms that generated the poetic fall of her skirt and tried to imagine the sheen and dimple of it all. Fiona, looking for her rubber, caught his sidelong gaze and Graham hastily returned to maligning Brenda's sturdy thigh.

Although Graham was in love with Fiona he hardly regarded her as attainable. He had never taken her out; had never walked down the street with her; had never even had a real conversation with her. Their greatest intimacy had in fact been on his first day in the class.

'One of the other students will show you all about cleaning brushes,' the principal had said, when the formalities of enrolment and general instructions were over. And so, at the end of the day, when Graham discovered Fiona, his senior by a term, at the sink he had asked her to show him about cleaning brushes. She had looked startled, almost affronted, but then she had taken a brush from his hand and shown him how to clean it, working the soap into the bristles with slim, muscular fingers. Graham's knees had trembled at the sight; his tongue had stuck to the roof of his mouth when he tried to thank her, and he had been unable to speak to her ever since.

Now he drew with a desperate thrust of the chalk, trying to force the shape into the paper. As he stabbed and smudged he lusted after Fiona. But if it was so hard to talk to her it was inconceivable that she would ever look openly into his face, letting him read her thoughts – let alone that she should permit him to discover those parts of her body that he could hardly believe she had discovered for herself. He felt the life class was something of an outrage to a girl like that, forcing her to acknowledge the facts demonstrated by Brenda's frank anatomy.

He drew worse, groping for conversational openings to use when the class ended. He reminded himself that most things seemed impossible till you did them. He wondered if he should suggest that they had lunch together. They could go to the White Hart, which had a rather superior lounge-bar but was not too expensive. He could do it casually, glancing over to her as they collected their things:

'Care for a spot of lunch?'

– No, that would be too sudden; too obviously planned. First something like:

'Drawing's quite tiring, isn't it?'

She would make a very cool reply, of course, like, 'Do you think so?' He would laugh, gather up his things and take three steps towards the door, then, as an afterthought:

'Care for a spot of lunch?'

Perhaps . . .

'Care for a spot of lunch?' It was Julian, wearing that corny neckerchief tucked in his shirt collar.

'All right.' Fiona scrambled her things together while Julian smirked and looked at her drawing. Then, with a nod to Graham, he led her off. Graham reflected that there was still tomorrow but, seeing Julian's hand laid lightly on Fiona's jewel of a hip to guide her through the door he longed for some 'pull', some hold that would bring her flank submissively under his palm. In his despair he almost embarked on childish imaginings of heroic deeds done before her eyes and preferably to save her life.

In the afternoon it was sculpture. The atmosphere was entirely different from that of the painting studio. Archie, the tutor, had spent some time in Paris and liked to think he re-created the atmosphere of an *atelier*. To that end he usually contrived to be drunk after lunch, and retired for long periods into his small den, from which he occasionally emerged to draw attention to some principle of form, grasping and moulding generous chunks of the surprised model to illustrate his verbal exposition – though that was unambiguous.

But this particular afternoon Archie was sober, and announced he would demonstrate the taking of a plaster mould from a clay figure. Brenda, who modelled for sculpture too, was therefore unemployed for the time being and sat in her wrap on the edge of the turntable on which she usually posed, smoking.

The class gathered round Archie and the clay figure. Graham looked for Fiona, but neither she nor Julian was to be seen. Sulkily, he watched as Archie mixed plaster that enveloped his hands like white gloves. But soon he had become fascinated by the so easy-looking underhand flick that sent skeins of plaster seeking their appointed place in the nooks and crevices of the clay. One had to admire old Archie's technique.

'Now, we remove these lightly fixed clay walls we built to keep the plaster to the first half of the figure . . . '

Archie's plaster-covered hands eased away the flaccid clay strips to reveal a cross-section of the plaster that now covered half the model.

'Make some location-marks . . . like that . . .,' he gouged the plaster with a spatula, '. . . that helps later on, when you come to put the two halves of the mould together – and apply little wedges of clay. They're to help you open the mould. Now –' he eyed Fiona and Julian, who had just sidled in '– we must put a clay wash on this plaster edge, to keep the two halves of the mould distinct.'

Graham caught sight of Fiona, looking like a tourist fascinated by local customs as Archie formed a small bowl out of clay, put a little water in it and stirred up a grey paste which he painted on to the exposed edge of the half-mould. Then he set about flicking plaster on to the other half of the figure. It was all beautifully simple and methodical.

Finally, the two halves of the mould were gently prised apart. Archie directed a jet of water to wash out the fragments of clay and reveal the inner surface of the mould. The students crooned admiration of the plaster contradiction that implied the original. Under the jet the clay slid away from the negative of a face.

'Can you do a life mask the same way?' asked Sammy Fish, the technical enthusiast.

'Same principle,' said Archie, puffing authentic boulevard atmosphere from his Gitane. 'You have to oil the model first, that's all.'

'What about the hair?'

'Cover it up, or work Vaseline into it so the plaster won't stick.'

'And you put straws up the nose?'

'That's right. You should let the others try it on you,' and Archie choked on his cigarette as he chuckled.

Sammy was fascinated. He cooed over the perfection of the moulds, his sharp nose almost touching the plaster. Even Graham was quite cheerful in the end, since he noticed that Fiona and Julian did not leave together.

But he did not take Fiona to lunch the next day, either. This time it was Brenda who prevented him, by falling asleep. When Maurice called 'Thank you, Brenda,' at the end of the drawing session, Brenda remained motionless. 'Time, Brenda, thank you!' Maurice called again, and Sammy Fish tiptoed across to within a couple of feet of Brenda and piped 'Cooee!'

Brenda still slept. At least, she looked as if she slept.

'Perhaps she's fainted,' said Sammy, looking at Seamus, but Seamus was engrossed and would not be disturbed.

'Try the kiss of life,' tittered Polly.

'Dead!' shouted someone else.

'Please stop that!' snapped Maurice, and he walked over to the recumbent girl. His hand hovered as he hesitated over shaking a naked shoulder, and he was as startled as anyone else when Fiona, on her way out of the room, delivered a sound smack to the broadest surface available. 'Wake up, Brenda!' she called, and was gone.

'Ow! That hurt, you cheeky bitch!' Brenda sat up rubbing her backside, nearly enveloped Maurice with herself in her gown as she flung it on, and strutted off to her box in a flurry of drapery and indignant pink heels. She could be heard muttering about stuck-up ninnies as she thumped and snapped elastic inside.

But by the afternoon Brenda seemed to have got over it. She even grinned when Sammy said he could still see the mark, and she showed no sign of resentment when Fiona clattered in on high-heeled boots, hanging up her coat to reveal a flowing envelope of sleek wool. Polly eyed the outfit before it disappeared under a smock, and pulled a wry face at Brenda, but Brenda only shrugged.

They were painting, that day. In her smeared man's shirt that she used as an overall, Polly, smudge-faced, looked as if she were in the middle of home decorating. But she was enjoying herself, and her boldly juxtaposed colours had a lively interplay. Seamus laid in a sombre foundation that declared Brenda's back unequivocally as squarer, thicker and meatier than anyone else's version. Graham struggled, less happy with paint than with pencil. His canvas was niggling and muddy. It had none of Polly's colour or Seamus's strength. Exasperated with the drab, sticky paste Graham stood back from his work and the cry that rang through the studio might have been a declaration of his despair.

'Aooh!'

Everyone looked at Fiona.

'Bugger!'

The shock was such that no one laughed. Fiona had taken off her smock and thrown it on the floor. Now she was twisting about, her hands held before her in helplessness as she inspected her svelte flanks, where weals of broken ochre and orange criss-crossed the expensively muted tones of the wool.

Polly picked up the smock and turned it out to reveal the clots of paint on the inside.

'Perhaps you laid it down on a palette,' she said. 'I did that once.'

'In this place there's paint everywhere,' said Seamus, whose dripping table bore him out.

Fiona huffed her exasperation and Polly found a clean rag. She borrowed Graham's expensive genuine turps and took Fiona to the washroom to clean her up.

'What happened?' asked Brenda, craning over her shoulder.

'Oh, that lovely cashmere!' she said, when they explained. 'What a shame!'

Wednesday morning passed uneventfully. Fiona was in her oldest clothes – a denim jump-suit that Graham found replete with gratifying information. Like Brenda the day before, she seemed to have got over her upset. Graham was more relaxed, because he had decided that taking Fiona to lunch was not a good idea anyway. It would be far too formal and intense, even if she agreed to come. Instead, he must simply take every advantage of their natural contact as fellow students. He placed most of his hopes on sculpture which, with its coming and going to fetch clay, borrow tools, turn the model and so on, offered more scope than the private intensities of the painting studio.

But this afternoon Archie, having emerged from his den to frown at the assembling class, muttered that he had just remembered something and disappeared. Evidently yesterday's sobriety had to be compensated for. The students drifted away too, or hung about spoiling finished work by fiddling with it. Graham was glad to see that Julian was among those that vanished.

Seamus swore at the armature he was making and threw it aside in disgust. 'I can't see to it till Archie unlocks the welder,' he said.

Brenda sat on her turntable and smoked. She was getting bored.

'Why don't we cast Brenda?' asked Sammy Fish.

'Because no one's sculpted her yet,' said Polly.

'I mean a life cast.'

'A mask, you mean – with straws?' Polly was rather keen.

'Why not a full figure? Eh, Brenda? How'd you like that, then?'

'What, cover me in plaster?' said Brenda. 'Do you mind?' but she giggled as she said it.

'You'd be preserved for posterity!' said Sammy.

Brenda looked at Seamus. He shrugged, and Brenda knew that he rather liked the idea.

'We can start by doing your back,' said Sammy. 'And if it works we'll do the front.'

Brenda sniffed and made a show of reluctance. Eventually, she prepared to clamber on to the turntable: 'I hope you know what you're doing,' she said.

'Not up there,' said Sammy. 'And anyway, you'll have to be oiled first.'

'Oiled?' Brenda didn't like the sound of that.

'Olive oil would be best,' said Polly. 'We can get it at Braithwaites – it'll be ever so good for your skin, Brenda!' Polly was quite excited at the idea of making an exact facsimile of a living person. She grabbed her handbag and scurried off.

That settled it. Money was being spent. Sammy and Seamus got out the flat panel that was laid on the turntable for reclining poses and put it across two trestles in the casting room, conveniently near the plaster bin and the sink. They fetched the heaters through and Brenda, clutching her cup of instant coffee, plugged them in and adjusted their position. It would be a change, at least, she said with resignation. In fact, like Polly she was rather excited.

Polly returned breathless and clutching a large bottle of salad oil – a lot cheaper, she explained, and just as good. She and Brenda retired to the model's box while Sammy and Seamus laid out bowls and spatulas.

Graham concluded he was not wanted. Besides, Fiona was up in the clay room doing what looked like some home baking with a rolling pin and a slab of terracotta.

But just as he set off to join her, Polly emerged from the box and ushered out Brenda, gleaming and pink like a joint that had just warmed through in the oven. Graham was fascinated by the myriad points of hair that glinted on her oily flanks. Usually Brenda was very prudish about uncovering herself between poses, gravely sliding into her dressing-gown with the minimum of movement at each rest. Now, arms held out from her sticky sides, she unselfconsciously padded across the floor, giggling when she nearly lost her balance as her feet slithered on the tiles. Perhaps she didn't feel naked under all that oil; more likely, being a practical girl, she simply accepted the inevitable – she couldn't very well put on a dressing-gown, could she?

'Whatever's going on?' It was Fiona, a striped businessman's shirt over her jump-suit, at the top of the steps to the clay room.

'We're going to cast Brenda,' said Polly. 'Want to help?'

'I think there's enough of you already,' said Fiona, with one of her downturned smiles. She clattered off in the clogs she wore for sculpture and turned back in the doorway to call gaily, 'I hope you know what you're doing!'

'Never fear,' said Seamus, dismissively.

Graham drifted up the steps after Fiona. This was an opportunity he couldn't let slip, he sternly told himself.

'Aren't you joining in the fun?' asked Fiona.

Graham shrugged. 'They're a bit childish,' he said.

'I don't know, it'll be interesting to see how they get on,' said Fiona, busy with her rolling-pin again.

'What are you doing?'

'It's going to be a relief.' She nodded to the drawing that lay on the bench. 'But this clay isn't easy to work . . . ' She pushed the hair out of her eyes with the back of her hand, and smiled at him as she puffed.

At the smile, Graham felt his knees weaken again.

137

'I'll knead it for you if you like,' he said.

'Would you? You are sweet!'

Hoping he wasn't making a fool of himself, Graham faced the clay that Fiona had willingly abandoned to him. He bounced it about to bring it to a nice lump, then he raised it high above his head and flung it down on the bench as he had seen a Japanese potter do in a film.

'Oh, that should do the trick,' said Fiona. Then, as he turned the clay and repeated the operation, 'Don't hurt yourself.'

Graham smiled in embarrassment and raised the clay again. Fiona wandered over to the open door leading down to the casting room, leaned on the jamb and lit a cigarette. Brenda's voice could be heard complaining that the board was hard, '– ooh! And it's cold!'

Graham imagined the shining body wobbling into place and adjusting itself stickily. Then he concentrated on thumping the clay – another dozen times should do it. Fiona leaned in the doorway, smoking and looking down into the casting room. When Brenda wailed that the plaster was icy, she gave her down-drooping grimace again, with a sort of snorting sound that Graham felt was for his benefit.

'It'll get warmer,' he heard Sammy say. 'Plaster generates heat as it sets – you'll soon be as warm as –' his words were drowned by Brenda's anger, followed by another wail, presumably caused by another application of plaster.

'Can't you warm the water?'

'We're using warm water for the next lot,' said Polly's voice. 'Now, let's make sure all your hair's inside the cap . . . '

There were more muted complaints from Brenda, a cry of 'Watch that edge – it's running everywhere,' from Seamus, and a firm 'Here, let me do that,' from Polly.

'That should just about do it,' said Graham, thumping the clay down for the last time.

'What? – Oh, you are a dear!' Fiona lingered for a moment to finish her cigarette and then strolled over to him. 'Do you like my design?'

'It's nice,' said Graham, 'but perhaps you ought to thicken up the forms a bit – you know, for a relief . . .'

Fiona bent over the drawing beside him and her hair brushed

his cheek. She smelt delicious, but Graham, afraid that the kneading might have made him sweaty, drew back. Fiona reached out for her pencil and her exquisite upper arm printed a gentle pressure on his shoulder that he tried to fix in his mind for ever. Now was the moment for seizing and kissing her.

'What on earth . . . ?' Fiona turned to him in astonishment. From the casting room Brenda was shouting – almost sobbing – Polly was squealing and Seamus and Sammy were issuing commands and countermands. Graham followed Fiona to the doorway. Down in the casting room, amid shallow lakes of spilt plaster, Polly, Seamus and Sammy were struggling to lift an enormous white mass off the bitterly complaining Brenda. Graham hurried to lend a hand, and with a sucking, lipsmacking sound the plaster came away. They carried it across to the bench, and Brenda, pinker than ever, rose on her hands and knees and accepted the gown that Polly offered – regardless of the oil – before clambering down.

'It was so heavy!' she complained. 'And it was getting hot, too.'

'I told you it would warm up,' said Sammy.

'Well, I've had enough!' said Brenda. 'Oh, I say!' She had caught sight of the mould from her back, which Sammy and Seamus had just turned the right way up. It was indeed a rather handsome object. The negative accentuated the waist and did the fullest justice to the swell of hip below it. The deep cleft of the spine was reproduced as a sturdy rib, flanked by the gently defined hollows of the shoulder-blades.

'It's terrific!' said Sammy.

Graham peered at the mould, which seemed to demonstrate the facts the more emphatically by its reversal of them. Brenda, fussed and given tea by Polly, was rather proud of herself, and forgot her sufferings in anticipation of the final result. It would be funny to stand face to face with oneself – not some sculptor's version, but oneself, exactly as one was. It was the sort of thing you'd like to be able to show your grandchildren when you were old.

Seamus and Sammy trimmed up the edges of the half-mould, cut register marks and reinforced it with more plaster on the outside. They they returned it, hollow side up, to the trestles and waited till Brenda was ready. Presently, she stubbed out her cigarette and came to confront the empty mould. She stood, her gown half off, and hesitated.

'How do I get in?'

'Just hop up,' said Sammy. He and Seamus held the mould steady. Brenda clambered up and offered her bottom to its matrix. She raised a foot and wobbled; Graham went to replace Seamus, who helped Polly ease Brenda down into the mould. Her pink flanks shimmied their way into the plaster.

'It's a tight fit,' croaked Brenda, then shook with laughter. 'Now I know what it feels like to be an Egyptian mummy!'

'Attagirl!' said Sammy.

'Well done!' said Polly.

'Right!' said Seamus, purposefully, and he began sprinkling plaster into a bowl of water. Meanwhile, Sammy carefully laid a piece of string across Brenda's shins, just below the knee.

'What's that for?' asked Polly.

'It's to divide the top half into sections. You pull it through the plaster just before it sets – like cutting cheese – I looked it up!'

Under his supervision Polly stretched another string across Brenda's stomach and yet another, to the accompaniment of much eye-rolling from the victim, across her neck.

'It isn't necessary, but it makes it easier,' explained Sammy.

'Plaster's ready!' Seamus was impatient.

'Is it warm this time?' asked Brenda. 'Oh, no! I like it warmer than that! U-ugh!' The plaster ran over her legs and dribbled over the bottom half of the mould to thicken the mess on the floor.

Sammy scraped the runnels away with a spatula. 'Don't be in such a hurry with the next lot,' he told Seamus. 'Let it get thicker before you pour it.'

Graham tore his eyes off the spectacle and turned back to try to recover lost ground with Fiona. But he found she had come down from the clay room and now she strolled past him to smile encouragingly at Brenda. Polly welcomed her with a grin and dipped a finger in the next bowl of plaster.

'It's pretty warm – but I think it'll be all right.'

Brenda murmured approval as the thick warm mass was

poured over her hips. 'That's better,' she said.

Seamus smoothed the plaster that now covered her from the waist down.

'Now the string!' said Sammy. He grasped each end of the first string, the one at Brenda's knees, and pulled it through the plaster with the gesture of a showman. The still-viscous paste closed again as the string passed through it. 'Too soon!' muttered Sammy. 'It doesn't really matter,' he reassured Brenda.

They poured more plaster, blanketing Brenda to the chest. Sammy tested the second string, pulled it, and triumphantly pointed to the neat cut it left in the setting mass. 'How's that for timing?'

But the next bit was going to be tricky. Fortunately, Brenda's nose was a turned-up affair with round nostrils that accepted the straws easily and let them emerge at the right angle. Polly held them in place until the plaster was ready.

'Right, shut your eyes, Brenda!'

It had been agreed that Brenda's right hand should be kept free so that she could signal with it if anything went wrong – the hand could always be cast later. Now she clenched her fist.

The sight of plaster being poured over a face is mildly horrific. Graham drew back a little and Seamus, hurrying for more plaster, told him to stand out of the way. Polly went to wash out a bowl, and Sammy peered at his string, watching for the moment when the plaster lost its wet shine – the signal that it was just right for cutting. Fiona, alone by the head, peered at the white mass, and experimentally poked it.

'Out of the way!' cried Seamus, and Fiona leapt aside in exaggerated haste as another coat of plaster flopped on to the head-end. Then she clattered back to the clay room.

'Now!' yelled Sammy, and pulled his string. It cut the plaster, but only slowly, and about halfway through it stuck. The combined efforts of Sammy and Seamus could move it no further.

'Too late. It's because the water was warm – it accelerates the setting. But it doesn't really –'

'Look!' screamed Polly, who had returned from the sink. 'Get her out quick!'

Brenda's exposed hand was frantically clenching and un-clenching.

'Perhaps she can't breathe!' Polly scraped at the place where the face must be, but the plaster was already set hard. 'She's suffocating!' Polly whimpered, clawing ineffectually.

'Don't panic,' Sammy was brisk and purposeful, 'just lift the top off – wedges, Seamus.' They hurriedly jammed wooden wedges into the places Sammy had thoughtfully provided. But the first wedge crumbled the plaster in its immediate neighbour-hood without opening the mould, and under Seamus's hammer-ing the second sank in until Sammy was terrified that it might be piercing Brenda's side. There was still no sign of a crack opening along the line where the two halves joined.

'Christ!' Sammy was aghast. 'We forgot the clay wash!'

The implication took a moment to sink in. It was that the two halves of the mould, unseparated by any film of clay, would have fused into one. Brenda was imprisoned in a solid case of plaster.

Her hand was now fluttering even more frantically, tearing at whatever was within reach. Polly sobbed and tore at the white mass with her nails.

'She may just have panicked,' said Sammy. He and Seamus and Graham thrust their fingers into the gaps left by the wedges and tried to pull the mould open. The whole mass lifted off the board, slipped from their grasp and fell back. One of the trestles collapsed and everything crashed to the floor. The plaster broke in great chunks and Brenda's rump appeared, dusty now, like a nascent Galatea.

'Fetch a hammer, for Christ's sake!' It was Archie, returned and breathing heady fumes and rage. They clawed the white head-end over on to what the exposed middle told them must be its back. Sammy came running with a lump hammer from the carving shed, and Archie gave the plaster a crack that sent Polly's hands to her own head in horror. A section of bathing cap and a shoulder were exposed. Another couple of blows, and Archie gently levered the broken pieces from Brenda's ashen face.

'It went up her nose!' wailed Polly and, indeed, the chunk of plaster that carried the print of Brenda's perfunctory snout did show no trace of straws, but two half-inch projections reproduced the inside of her nostrils.

Archie had pulled the plaster away from Brenda's shoulders and chest. 'Phone for an ambulance,' he said, and started artificial respiration. Polly pushed him away and began mouth-to-mouth resuscitation. The ambulance arrived just after Brenda started independent breathing. She was moving her head about and moaning by the time they were ready to get her on to the stretcher. The ambulanceman who lifted the blanket that Archie had fetched from the first-aid room let it fall back with an apology when he saw the patient had no clothes on. His companion, who bent to grasp the feet, was mystified at what he encountered and lifted his end of the blanket to stare in bewilderment at the block of plaster from which Brenda's thighs emerged. Archie stepped forward with his hammer, but the man waved him away.

'Hands off! The doctors'll see to it!' The veins stood out on his forehead as he tried to lift half of Brenda and half a hundredweight of damp plaster. Seamus helped him. As they pushed the stretcher into the ambulance the man confided, 'Last week it was a feller boiled, in a brewery!'

Archie cursed the students and set them to work clearing up. While Seamus and Sammy scraped plaster off the floor, Graham helped Polly clean the sinks and bowls and put away the spatulas. When he took some modelling tools back to the clay room, he found Fiona staring out of the window. She turned her face away as he came in, and he thought it rather unfair that she should blame him for the goings-on downstairs. Basely, he tried to dissociate himself from the disaster by echoing her disapproval.

'That was a stupid thing to do, wasn't it?'

'What?' said Fiona, in a low voice.

'Down there,' said Graham.

Fiona turned round. What astonished Graham more than the tears that were streaming down her face was her open-mouthed look of terror. Suddenly she was a girl like Polly – or even Brenda – only skinnier and sweating with fear.

'I only meant it as a joke – just to frighten her! I just twitched the straws – I wasn't to know they couldn't get her out!' She blurted and honked the words, and when Graham raised his hands in a gesture, half of embarrassed self-protection, half of sheer bewilderment, she tottered forward between them and sobbed wetly on his collar.

He instinctively pattted her neck and assured her it was all right. Brenda would be all right. No one had noticed. She had better forget about it. She disengaged herself and accepted a handkerchief to mop her blotchy face. Sadly, he reflected that he supposed this meant he had a hold on her, but it was not, after all, a very nice feeling.

'Don't worry,' he said, and turned to go.

'You won't –'

'Oh, forget it,' and he hurried down the stairs.

The Proposal

'Yes', said George into the telephone. 'Yes, well . . . '

Behind him a door creaked; he glanced round and saw Mrs Smith, like a mountaineer at last reaching the South Col, emerging from the basement.

'No,' he said into the telephone, conscious that Mrs Smith, her head shaking slightly and her shoulders hunched, was trekking across the hall to the foot of the main staircase.

'No, it's not that, it's just that . . . ' George watched Mrs Smith's feet making the acquaintance of each tread of the stairs in turn.

'Don't be silly!' he told the telephone.

With a final flexing of thick ankles and a weary sigh, Mrs Smith's feet attained the landing.

'Of course I'd rather be with you, but you know how it is . . . anyway, it will give us both time to think things through.'

The landing creaked; there was laboured breathing and the squeak of a duster.

'Of course I'm not going off you . . . No, that's absurd. It's just that I thought – '

Mrs Smith was descending the stairs again, dragging the duster down the handrail.

'I really can't go into it all now,' said George. 'Yes, it's pouring here too.' He looked at the stained-glass window above the telephone, where spots and runnels improved the coarse flower-shapes and droplets graced a chink where the glass was missing.

'Look, I'll be back by Tuesday. I'll ring you then.'

Mrs Smith, returned to the hall, was heading grimly for the front door.

'Don't be silly!' hissed George, and winced at the open door and the dust that blew in from the shaken duster. 'Look, I must go . . . No . . . All right then. 'Bye,' and he rang off as Mrs Smith closed the door.

He had not proposed. He had not proposed and Sally was now in a huff. She had expected it and he had meant to do it, but what with Mrs Smith and the rain – rain was always discouraging to enterprise.

And of course, to be perfectly honest he did have doubts – or rather, he was afraid he might have doubts later, which came to much the same thing. Sally as a wife? He had doubts about her chinline, and he had doubts when he thought he detected a concern for economy and for his moral welfare that seemed less than fun-loving. Could it be that all wives saw themselves to some extent *in loco parentis*?

But these were surely the last reactionary doubts that one always had before doing something – like the feeling of not wanting to go when packing for a holiday. It wasn't as if they were in the first throes of romantic love and carried away by physical longing. They had, after all, been living together for eleven months before he moved up here, and they still met nearly every weekend. Besides, they were neither of them – especially George – exactly in first youth.

All the same, on his way upstairs he continued to feel guilty. Then he became irritated with Sally for not looking for a job in the north. Perhaps she thought the separation would show him what he was missing and make him take steps to 'establish continuity of supply' as they said in the office. On the landing he thought about that fellow from her paper who was supposed to have cuddled her in the boathouse after nearly drowning her when his dinghy capsized. With his hand on the doorknob of his room he reminded himself that everyone spoke of George and Sally as a natural unit and joint invitations were a matter of course. They did get on remarkably well; no other girl seemed to find so many qualities in him and perhaps the chinline would improve with time. Because she was very trim generally . . .

He went downstairs and re-dialled. When she answered he smiled into the mouthpiece and said 'It's me again.'

'Oh,' she said.

'I was thinking. Perhaps I won't go to Suffolk.'

'Can't you ever make up your mind about anything?'

'Well, I thought – '

'I thought it was so important for you to see your father?'

'Well, what will you do if I go?'

'Go to the regatta on my own, I suppose.'

'You might crew for that idiot Alec, perhaps.'

'That's an idea.'

'Well, I would, if I were you.'

'I probably shall if he asks me.'

'OK, if that's what you want.'

There was silence from the other end.

' 'Bye,' he said, and rang off. He peered through the chink in the stained glass at rods of rain splashing into puddles on Mrs Smith's lawn. Fine weather for regattas. Behind him he heard the door to the basement close discreetly.

So instead of joining Sally in Gloucestershire, where their Saturday night would have been rendered almost connubial by the assurance of a languid revision on Sunday afternoon, George went to Suffolk to see his father. As he travelled eastwards, the sky expanded over a flattening earth, and slow-moving people turned mild coffin-faces to watch the train pass.

His father was pleased to see him and immediately set about getting a meal. George was not allowed to help, on the grounds of his incompetence. There was a way of doing everything, and only his father knew it. The place was spotless, but such standards could only be maintained by rigid method. It was a bit like the lonely white man in an outpost of Empire dressing for dinner because letting things slip a fraction might start the slide towards chaos, shame and degradation.

After the meal his father, relishing company, talked:

'Did you know Mr Deacon was in hospital?'

'No – well, perhaps you mentioned it.'

'He was in the next ward to me. I went to see him before I came out. He wasn't at all well.'

'Oh dear.'

'He didn't want to talk, so I just came away. Want a sweet?'

'No thanks.'

'What's that you're reading?'

George held up his magazine. 'Just a weekly.'

'Hm. Did you know Mrs Birrell was found dead?'

'No.'

'She'd been dead some time. The neighbours noticed. There's peppermints in that tin.'

'No thanks.'

'Have a toffee.'

'Not just now.'

'Why not?'

George was reading about Soviet misbehaviour in Afghanistan, which reminded him of the retired Indian Army man who used to tell him stories about the North West frontier.

'How's Major Milne?' he asked.

'Been dead years. And his wife. She died before he did.'

'He was a good age, I suppose.'

'Over eighty, but she was younger. They both died of drink.'

It was unkind to come on a visit and then sit immersed in a magazine, so George suggested a walk up town, where he could buy tobacco.

Waiting for his father in the pedestrian precinct outside the new supermarket – into which he had been forbidden to follow, in case he should attempt to pay for something – George heard snatches of conversation.

'He was taken ill on the Tuesday, and on the Thursday I sent for the doctor . . . ' The speaker paused and drew back her head like a hen as she took ample breath. The story was going to be long and detailed. George moved out of earshot, but the precinct was full of voices:

'. . . of course, her marriage had broken down . . .' George imagined a desolate woman confronted with a marriage slumped at the kerbside – beds flat, baths leaking, passion run dry . . . He paced the front of the supermarket.

'It wasn't the kidneys that were at fault, oh, no!'

The recipient of this information nodded wisely. The kidneys were perfectly blameless – as glistening and rosily innocent as those on that dish in the butcher's window. George tried to locate the speaker's kidneys on her broad back; they were probably just about there, with a damaging crease right across them. He turned to pace back again.

'. . . they took her into the West Suffolk hospital and operated the same day. They had to take everything away . . . '

George saw his father along the street, talking to a man whose moustache was vaguely familiar. Catching sight of George, he waved goodbye to the moustache and came across.

'You know who that was?' And when George obviously did not: 'Mr Poole. Bad job about his son.'

'What happened to him?'

'Started a Country Food Centre where Robertson's fish shop used to be. Went down to the freezer centre to pick up some stock and fell down dead with a side of bacon.'

George crooned astonishment.

'We'll go back round by the bridges,' announced his father.

They went down through the old heart of the town, past the new Health Centre and the Garden Centre with its plaster urns and the Travel Centre that had replaced the tumbledown house that was supposed to be haunted. The Health Centre had flint panels set into its concrete frame in polite acknowledgement of the local tradition. For this had been a town of flint. Its humbler walls had been knobbly with rounded stones, their mushroom-coloured skin intact, set in a lime mortar so soft that small fingers could prise it away. Better quality work had the blue cut faces of the flints showing, and they could chisel your hands if you brushed too close. Eighteenth-century churches, and almshouses built without regard for dirt-cheap labour, had walls of regular dark blue cubes cut from the heart of the flint. They were potentially eternal. But now only fragments of the old walls remained round the gaps that marked the surprisingly small sites of remembered dwellings.

'That's Captain Long's,' said George's father, indicating a patch of scraped clay fronted by a doorstep. George looked round for the bit of high pavement ending in steps, where they used to sit and haggle over cigarette cards. It had gone.

They had reached the narrow junction beside Sir William

Partridge's gates, now labelled 'Partridge Memorial Home'. The cottage opposite still had roses on the trellis round the door.

'I always think PC Hardy's is a pretty house,' said George.

'What's that?'

'I said I always thought that was a pretty house.'

'Hmph!' His father pointed to the cottage. 'PC Hardy used to live there.'

'I know.'

'Dead, of course. Been dead years. Pretty place, though.'

'Yes,' said George.

On Sunday they visited the graveyard where George's mother was buried, and walked through the surrounding avenues of headstones. Here was the *nouveau riche* builder who went bankrupt. Here was Harry Lord the rag-and-bone man, whose cry had wandered over the town, approaching and receding like the call of a bird. Here was the man whose wife had found him with his throat cut – 'from ear to ear', of course – and the young woman who had been run over by a tank on the town bridge during the war. In a small enclosure stood the expensive but neglected stones of the now extinct Partridges. Mr Mole, whose bass had so impressed choirboy George with its low-frequency vibration just behind his own squeaking head, lay beside Old Tom. Tom, gnarled as his trees, lay beside the fat wife he used to lead out every Sunday, stiffly giving her his arm, banana fingers hanging red and embarrassed, without an axe to hold.

They were all here. People George had forgotten but who, if their names had been mentioned, he would have imagined still cheerfully delivering milk, or chopping up sides of beef, or offering a nice bit of cod with that curious nasal thickness common to fishmongers.

'Remember him?' His father pointed to a stone near the gate, and George did indeed remember Mr Stebbings, grinning with all his crooked teeth clamped round his pipe and leaning back in the wind as his wagon bounced and rumbled behind an enormous white stallion. Even though the beast struck sparks

150

with every crashing hoof, it seemed hardly more powerful than Mr Stebbings, in his thick cords and weskit.

'He was all shrivelled up at the end,' said George's father.

When it was time to go, his father insisted on seeing George to the station. Other people were already there, waiting on the patch where the bookstall used to stand. A familiar figure was concluding a narrative:

'. . . When the doctor came into the room afterwards he spoke to me. He said, "Your husband's body was full of poison, Mrs Ballard. There was nothing we could do – it wasn't the kidneys that were at fault . . . " '

'Well, there,' intoned her audience. 'Like that it was a happy release, then. Did you know my niece Lorna went back in on Friday? It was a black doctor – but very clever, they say. He put her on to antibiotics but he couldn't shift that polypus for her . . .'

The train came in. As the passengers looked for seats the signal rods jerked beside the track and George watched the station and his father swim slowly aside. He leaned out of the window and saw the familiar figure turn away and set off back to the empty house that had once contained a family.

As soon as he reached Mrs Smith's George telephoned Sally, fumbling over the numbers in his haste. He became anxious as the ringing tone went on and on.

'Hello?' Her voice. At last.

'Hello, I'm back. You all right?'

'Of course.' Of course. All limbs sound and articulating smoothly, skin unbroken, no cankers in the bud –

'How was your father?'

'Oh, fine, he's amazing. Look, I've been thinking . . .'

'Yes?' Her voice was quite clear – not a trace of decay bubbling from below.

'I think we should get married as soon as possible.' Every day would be a day gained.

'Well!' Surprised, she laughed. When she laughed she bared

151

part of her pink, healthy inside. He laughed too, and beamed at Mrs Smith, who had emerged from the basement carrying dead leaves in a vase.

'All right?' he asked the telephone.

'Why the hurry?'

George resolved to buy Mrs Smith some flowers. Fresh flowers were splendid. Besides, 'Gather ye rosebuds . . . '

'I just thought it was about time,' he said. 'All right?'

'I suppose so!' Sally laughed again, evidently delighted. Whenever she laughed her breasts shook very slightly, like apples on a tree.

'See you next weekend, then.'

'All right.'

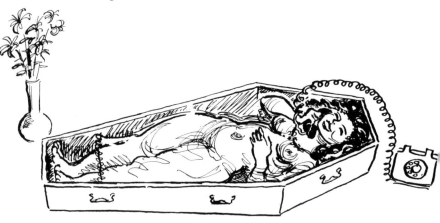

Schoolboy War

A great deal came across the field. One lunchtime it was a poor lost Dornier; it dived with popping engines out of the cloud, iron crosses splendidly evident, then pulled up and vanished again. John had just come home from school, where they had spent the morning in the shelters but been let out for dinner. That day it was snowing. It was raining when he saw the Heinkel from the town bridge, and sunny when he pointed out the perfect formation of Junkers Ju 88s, flying very high, to disbelieving adults who afterwards marvelled at the bombs on Stowmarket.

One Saturday a barrage balloon, escaped from Norwich, trailed wires and rumours of netted Messerschmitts through the poplars behind the pavilion and set men talking of the folly of leaving ATS girls in charge of anything. The balloon came, sagging and weary, threatening to settle on the cricket pitch, then disclosing lumbering speed as it passed overhead. The cables shrieked and sparked on the telegraph wires; dogs barked and so did men: 'Keep clear or it'll take your leg off!' The balloon swept away towards Bury St Edmunds like a great grey pig, its Mickey Mouse ears flopping half-deflated.

Now, with the sky swept clear of Heinkels and Dorniers and all those other bogey-man names, it was a Flying Fortress that came across the field. Not that anyone but women and small children called them 'Flying Fortresses' by then. The RAF, when it dallied with the first version, years before, had trimmed the name to 'Fortress', and that was current English usage. The Yanks just called them 'B17s'. This one cruised round the estate, banking to show its enormous MK II fin raised high like the poop of a galleon and the white letter 'H' large on its dun-coloured paint.

It passed out of sight and only the sound of its engines remained, an obscure muttering from the edge of the sky. Then it reappeared over the trees at the far side of the field, head-on and very low. The fuselage was a round nucleus in the middle of the straight wings, each one blobbed with two round engines. One could see the ball-turret bulging underneath and, as it drew nearer, the slotted chin-guns below the transparent nose.

As the blunt, old-fashioned wings swept overhead the engine sound reached a surging climax, then tumbled in pitch and intensity. The starboard outer wing was evidently a replacement, for it shone in the silver of unpainted aluminium, which was the way all the newer American planes were finished. The roar of engines had almost drowned the squeals from the garden next door but one. The Ainslie girls were there. No doubt they were the reason for this visitation. They had been sitting in deck-chairs, screaming and waving; now they scrambled up and shaded their eyes to watch as the Fortress climbed away and droned out of sight once more.

Then it came again. First the threatening rumble, then the wingtips above the trees and suddenly the whole thing leaping into sight like a child with its arms stretched wide. It rushed on them, and as it skimmed the telegraph poles someone could be seen waving from the navigator's position in the transparent nose.

The Ainslie girls screamed and waved again – the youngest lost all decorum and waved her legs instead of her arms as she lay back, ecstatic in her deck-chair as the great bulk passed over her. Then they all tore round to the other side of the houses and saw the top of the broad wings as the tail depressed over the backyards and the monster withdrew into its proper place, remote in the sky. By now everyone was outside. They watched the high-tailed profile drifting round behind the gasometer and the poplars and willows of the river. The sound of the engines faded.

'Reckon tha's all for today,' said old Mr Dunwich over the hedge, before he returned to his hoeing. The Ainslie girls hung about hopefully, then dropped into their chairs again.

Restlessly, they thumbed the copies of *Life* and *Saturday Evening Post* that American admirers had brought, unwrapped those excessively sweet Hershey bars and triggered each other's shrieks of laughter with hissed remarks, so that when the plane came for the third time it took them by surprise.

It came lower than ever, sinking till it seemed to flatten the grass as it roared – you knew it was roaring, though you couldn't hear it yet – across the cricket pitch.

'He's a-gorn to hit them wires!' shouted old Dunwich, flinging down his hoe and preparing to run. But the nose lifted just in time and the great machine swept overhead, every rivet evident.

The engines glinted potently in their nacelles. John's eyes devoured the blur of the airscrews – Hamilton Hydromatics – and his ears drank the mild sound of the Wright Cyclone radials – it was mild because the exhausts were muffled by the turbo-superchargers. He looked so fiercely, so eagerly, that in later recapitulation it seemed the plane had hung motionless for seconds as he absorbed its blunt wingtips, the visibly moving control surfaces, the projecting guns and the glimpsed head in the cockpit. The naked girl painted on the nose was a nuisance to be discounted as one gauged the flow of the aluminium panels.

John ran round to the back of the house and saw the departing shape bank to avoid St Anselm's tower. The Ainslie girls were still screaming. The youngest had jammed her fingers when her deck-chair collapsed and the others were falling on each other's necks in gleeful terror. Mother Culver was saying that if God had intended us to fly . . . and old Dunwich was stuffing shag into his pipe and shaking his head at his parsnips.

The boy hung about covertly. He really disapproved of the Yanks' vulgar display and was indignant at the naivety of these marvelling people. It had been impressive, of course – but it wasn't as if it were an Avro Lancaster. Now that would really have been something to wonder at.

The aerodromes had come one by one, with the town's casual

labourers being carried off in lorries to make brief fortunes laying runways at Honington, Wretham and Feltwell until it seemed that the place must be surrounded by a continuous ring of concrete. But at first there had been no runways; low-pressure tyres and sandy soil had enabled Wellingtons to land on grass by the light of oil lamps. The Yanks, with their miles of concrete and banks of electric lights far out into the fields, knew nothing of those heroic days.

Every afternoon in 1940 and 1941 there had come the trumpeting of engines: Bristol Pegasus being 'run up' across five or ten miles of flat fields and pines. At night there came the pulsing drone of regularly spaced departure and in the early hours people woke to the less regularly spaced sounds of return. John had marvelled that those engines had been working all the time he slept; valves dancing, gears humming. Sometimes a returning plane sounded strange, and once a rush to the window had been rewarded by the sight of flames moving slowly across the night sky.

The same timetable was now maintained by the deeper sound of the Lancasters' Rolls-Royce Merlins – four apiece. And in the daylight the American squadrons assembled, peopling the tolerant vastness of the East Anglian sky with tight formations of deep-bodied, narrow-winged Liberators and high-pooped Fortresses. But John still thought affectionately of the old Wellingtons with their sweet drone, and of the Czechs and Poles who had flown them so gaily. One had pulled a wing off over the goods station, trying to loop the loop; the sturdy geodetic frame that would absorb so much punishment could not quite rise to such a magnificent gesture.

He was reminded of the Wellingtons as he tramped across stubble ten miles from home, keeping in line with his father, the farm foreman and Miss Darcy. He had come for the ride in Miss Darcy's hunched Triumph Gloria – which she had never let rip – and because the farm bordered on airfield. It was disappointing, because where there had been Wellingtons there were now only Dakotas, lumbering in and out with freight. The pig-like

Marauders that had followed the Wellingtons had not stayed long. With their fat bellies, tiny wings and tricycle undercarriages they had landed alarmingly fast and had always been crashing. The Dakotas just walked on and off the ground and were hardly more exciting than railway trains.

'Look out!' shouted the foreman as a rabbit scuttled from a tussock at John's feet. The boy waved his .410 hopelessly; Miss Darcy lowered her instinctively raised twelve-bore, too well trained to fire along the line.

'Sorry,' John muttered, and tried to concentrate on the ground ahead. The tussocks were jungle and he was flying low in a tank-busting Hurricane IID – or better, swooping in an elliptically-winged Hawker Tempest, the twenty-four pistons of its doubly double-banked Napier Sabre straining to drive the mighty airscrew.

There was a rattling, whistling sound from overhead. John looked up and saw a bird diving vertically, wings arched and vibrating with speed. It pulled out of its dive within a yard of the ground and climbed back, zigagging as if to avoid *flak*. Then it toppled and dived again, like the Junker 87 *Stukas* over Crete.

'Snipe,' said the foreman. 'You stick to rabbits, boy.'

John had thought it was a lapwing. Lapwings always reminded him of *Stukas* anyway, with their cranked wings – cranked the wrong way, but on the same principle. To him every bird represented a different kind of plane. Two magpies rowed across the field, nose-down and long tails trailing. They were obviously Handley-Page Hampdens. And there went a pigeon; pigeons were De Havilland Mosquitoes. Miss Dixon fired and got a puff of features, but the bird flew on. Pigeons were fast like Mosquitoes, and their grey plumage was like the latest daylight camouflage that Mosquitoes wore. But pigeons could take punishment; the shot from a .410 could just bounce off the thick down on their breasts, according to Pilger. Mosquitoes – Pilger described them as two engines tied together with glue and balsawood – were more delicate. Still, the Yanks had nothing like them. A Mosquito carried the same bomb load as a Fortress with far less fuss – only two men instead of ten – and much faster.

The pigeon reached the trees in safety. Sometimes when they were shot they climbed furiously before cartwheeling to the ground. Pilger said they did that when they were hit in the lungs and gasping for breath. It was as if a wounded pilot pulled back on the stick, then slumped forward dead. There went another pigeon, head down and urgent, like its wooden *alter ego* that sped, Merlins singing, speed in every line, a lean sports car unconfined by roads and removed from the gross earth.

Back home that evening he walked the dog on the field and watched a Lancaster up from Feltwell, probably on test before tonight's raid. Its drone was insistent – it was made by four Merlins pounding away, after all – and the sound boomed and reverberated as the throttles were opened. He thought he could see how it gathered speed. The pilot would be juggling the levers now . . . ah, yes, the engines settled back to a synchron-ized beat. As the heavy machine banked the chipped spots in the black night camouflage flashed in the low sun and the squadron letters showed dull red along the side. It must be the best in the world: eight tons of bombs – ten, with modified bomb-doors, and a load of clumsy radar. The Yanks had nothing like it.

He had never seen inside a Lancaster. Occasionally, the shy gods who flew in them walked among mortals in the street. He had even spent an afternoon beside one, a friend of Pilger's, sitting under the hedge at the edge of the field, dangling their feet in the almost obliterated Home Guard trenches as they watched a cricket match. The airman wore a winged 'N' at his breast and had come to visit one of the Ainslie girls, but she was out with a Yank. He would not confess to navigating a Lancaster though Pilger, whose brother had been at school with him, knew that he did.

John would love to see inside a Lancaster, but that was impossible. One couldn't get near a British aerodrome. But tomorrow he was going to stay with Pilger, whose father had a farm alongside an American airfield and who claimed to wander about it as he pleased. That was at least something.

As he turned to go back indoors a tomtit crossed his path in bursts of fluttering, like a First-war Sopwith Camel 'blipping' its motor. (Gnome rotary engines had no throttles; only an off-on switch.)

It was delicious to be actually on an aerodrome. John pedalled behind Pilger, who rode in lordly fashion, leaning back with one hand casually in the middle of his flashy dropped handlebars. They drifted with the indirection of butterflies between the low-slung, high-finned Fortresses dispersed on their patches of concrete. It was delectable to be familiar with these great beasts that held acquaintance with the upper air. They skirted the perforated gun-barrels that projected from rear turrets; they passed under wings, avoiding the chubby tyres and blunt propeller blades. They lingered where knots of men crouched under rounded bellies: bomb-doors whined open; stubby American bombs were winched in.

It would be unthinkable on a British station. You'd never even get near the gate. But the Americans took no notice. This was the first time John had seen them on their own ground. They were all over the town, of course, their cheeky uniforms showing off their curiously rounded backsides. They seemed very boyish and made a lot of self-consciously happy noise. Girls giggled and shrieked in their company, and grew plump on Hershey bars.

Here the Yanks grinned less, moving with unhurried purposefulness about the muddy concrete and grass. Everything about them seemed more or less mud-coloured – their denim overalls, their boots, their long-peaked fatigue caps, their faces, the jeeps in which they sprawled extravagantly akimbo – even their aeroplanes were mud-coloured, except for the latest deliveries, which stood naked in dew-beaded silver under the dull East Anglian sky.

The aerodrome was a great expanse of fields bound into one by grey concrete runways that disappeared into the distance. Crossing the end of the runways one found there were joints in the concrete with grass pushing through, and streaks of oil and

159

tyre-rubber where the planes touched down. The Fortresses were dispersed between Nissen huts and occasional clumps of trees that had been allowed to remain. Above the sound of passing trucks and sporadically raised transatlantic voices there came the occasional crescendo of an engine being tested, or the rising drone of a Fortress taking off.

Pilger was clearly trying to make this visit as memorable as possible. Already they had retired to a small pit in the woods and let off an incendiary bomb. It was a present from a Yank, and intended for destroying a plane that had crash-landed in enemy territory – you were supposed to put it on the wing, over the petrol tanks. The boys had put it on some stones and turned the knob on top according to the instructions on the side. The small canister sat for a second or so, then turned red-yellow and melted into a pool of fire. Pilger picked up an old shovel and fed it into the glowing puddle. That had been an interesting start to the day; better than carbide bombs in the bike sheds, anyway.

Now they arrived at a dispersal point where some Americans Pilger knew were working on a brand new Fortress. John observed them at close quarters. They were plump. Even the thin ones were plump in places, with nests of fat on cheeks, in the corners of mouths and under jawbones. British servicemen would seem puny by comparison. And these fellows moved with a broadness of gesture – an absence of restraint – that was oddly different from the movements of skinny British soldiers in nailed boots and shapeless battledress.

The American spoke slowly, with something so akin to the nasal East Anglian whine as to be almost homely. They uttered lots of nuggety, worldly-wise phrases that suggested an original turn of mind until you realized they were all stock expressions. The rest of their talk was as stumbling as that of British soldiers, who were fluent only in profanity. John discovered that these people worked their own vein of obscenity just as obsessively.

The boys hung about embarrassed, as the Americans, who were taking a break, rolled about and grabbed at each other in sexual horseplay. They were overt and unsubtle in everything they did. They spat; they peed at the edge of the concrete without bothering to turn away; their movements at work were large and effective, but somehow immodest. They were surprisingly industrious, and yet there was something of the untutored boy – something almost babyish – about them.

The leader of the ground crew, who Pilger called 'Hank', got up and started work again. With a spraygun he directed a jet of liquid at the flaps on the trailing edge of the wing. As it struck the metal there came the familiar pungent reek of petrol.

'You Limeys clean your ships with gas?' asked Hank. He was trying to be friendly.

'I don't think so,' said John. Then he added, primly: ' I don't think we could spare the fuel.' He wondered if he should explain what the posters had been saying for years – that imports cost lives – but decided not to.

'Look there!' said Pilger, and pointed to where a column of red and yellow flames had mushroomed from a dispersal pad a few hundred yards away. 'It's all right, they've wheeled the plane away, see? When they've finished spraying they just set light to the petrol that's lying about to get rid of it.' The boiling mass of flame was a coloured version of newsreels of plane-crashes and bombardments. But the excitement was short-lived, and as a final smear of dark smoke drifted away the dispersal point reappeared quite undamaged.

John turned back to the plane beside him. He had already examined it from every angle, peering up at the glazed nose and the chin-turret – they added that after the disastrous Schwein-furt raid – and crouching to examine the ball-turret under the rear belly. The gunner had to curl up like a foetus, and it was unpleasant to speculate on the likely trajectory of any cannon-shells that might come his way as he huddled, presenting his backside to the enemy and firing between his feet.

Now John approached the open rear door, just ahead of the tailplane, and looked in on the secret world of aluminium and Plexiglas. The stringers and ribs that framed the cylindrical fuselage were exposed; the tradename of the alloy sheet that covered them was repeatedly stencilled across it surface. There, a little ahead, was the round bulge of the ball-turret – most of it was outside, of course, hanging like a scrotum under the plane's belly. There was a gangplank of yellow wood; pale green oxygen cylinders; then the waistguns, slung in the square gunports with a cowboy casualness and looped with belts of ·5 cartridges. Immediately under them were sheets of armour-plate: cissy! No wonder Fortresses carried so few bombs. He'd read somewhere that the only armourplate in a Lancaster was a simple disc behind the pilot's head.

He leaned further into the doorway, feet almost off the ground, and peered along the aeroplane, inhaling its strange, exciting smell. He could look through the radio operators's compartment – there was another gun there, but you couldn't see it from here – right along to the bomb-aimer's position, bright with the light that poured in through the nose. There was no sign of the secret bombsight the Yanks were so proud of.

Above, on a sort of shelf under which you would have to duck to get into the nose, were the seats of the pilot and co-pilot and, glimpsed between them, the dials and levers of the controls. He squirmed for a better view: there were the flight instruments, there were the throttles, and –

'Come outa there, bo-oy!'

John returned to the world of earth and grass and mortal men, to the tedious sounds of birds chirping and Pilger's impatience.

'They're getting fed up with you,' said Pilger. He went over to his bike through the first spots of rain. 'Come on. We can go to the pictures.'

They pedalled through the gathering drops and reached the large hut that served as camp cinema just before the rain really started. Gus Harman was there, smoking Camels and choking. Fat, tow-headed Gus, whose father farmed at Lopham, was not very bright, but he tried to impress. He said they should have come last week, when there had been a striptease show. John listened to his garment-by-garment account with fascinated disbelief.

'There's a prostitute in a hut round by "Yankee Doodle",' Gus whispered as the lights dimmed.

'I know,' said Pilger. 'That's why we haven't been round there.'

'Button up, down there,' murmured an American sitting with

his feet on the back of John's seat. They buttoned up and watched Bob Hope.

It was still raining when they came out and rode off between the hunched Americans loping for shelter. Gus left them at the camp gates, threatening to see them tomorrow. As his smoker's cough receded towards Lopham they bowed over their handlebars and made for Pilger's place, lifting their feet to avoid the spray when American trucks, standing high on their big wheels, lurched past. As he pedalled John carefully recapitulated the interior of a Fortress. As the rain penetrated his collar he found he was almost fond of the thick wings and round bellies, and as the water trickled down his back he decided that it hadn't been a bad day.

But the next day Pilger was unwell – a chill, pronounced his mother, which served him right for getting soaked. John felt in the way. In the afternoon, probably to everyone's relief, he pedalled off to the airfield. Gus was waiting at the gate, combining sitting on his bike with leaning on the sentry-box in an attitude of almost American angularity. The ground about him was littered with cigarette ends, though he said he hadn't been waiting long.

Like Pilger, Gus knew his way about the airfield and was fluent in American. He led off round the perimeter track, calling 'Hi fellas!' and 'What say, Joe?' to the Americans as he passed. Finally, he pulled up under the wing of a Fortress. It was another new one, left unpainted except for an anti-dazzle patch in front of the cockpit and a red scrawl of 'Yankee Doodle' on the nose.

'There's the hut,' said Gus, hoarsely, pointing to an ordinary Nissen hut that was immediately made gravid with vice.

'How do you know she's there?' asked John.

'Ah-ha!' Gus was elaborately knowing, looking at John from under drooped eyelids as he drew a Camel from its packet with his lips, as the Yanks did.

But Yankee Doodle was quite as interesting as the proximity of sin, and her most attractive feature was a jagged hole in one wing. John peered at it and sniffed the faint, flinty smell that clung to the torn edges of metal.

'Was it anti-aircraft fire?' he asked an American who jumped down from inspecting the damage from above.

'Guess so!' said the American. 'Now get along you-all,' and he walked across to the next dispersal point, where he said something to the men who were busy spraying a Fortress. They laughed. One of them joined him and they walked to the hut, hands in pockets, sidling into each other and staggering in little bouts of laughter as they went.

Gus pedalled slowly towards the hut, stopped a little way off and stood straddling his crossbar. He choked over his cigarette, but silenced himself to listen when there came the sound of a girl's voice, giggling and protesting. John sniggered and shuffled his bike forward, but Gus threw his cigarette down and tugged him back. 'Let's be going,' he said, and turned his bike round. John reluctantly followed. There was a burst of ribald cheering from the hut and two more men downed tools beside the plane and hurried across. Only the man with the spraygun remained, and when there came another burst of cheering, this time accompanied by yipping noises, he put that down and loped to the hut. As he went inside someone gave a yell of welcome.

John turned aside from following Gus to visit the plane the men had left. Like all the Fortresses on the airfield it had an 'H' painted on its enormous fin. It was drab-camouflaged, with one new wing left unpainted. A naked girl was sprawled along the nose. John laid down his bike and walked to the edge of the concrete pad, looking rather patronizingly at the monster now that he had it on the ground. A week ago, terrifying the Ainslie girls, it had been really impressive, but now he knew all about Fortresses, and could afford to treat them casually. The smell of petrol-spraying hung in the air.

'What are you hanging about for?' Gus joined him. For once he was not smoking.

'Just looking.'

There was more cheering and a drumming of feet from the hut.

164

'Come on,' said Gus.

'Just a minute.' John refused to think about why he was waiting. He knew it had something to do with the Ainslie girls and the low-flying Fortresses and the splendour of Lancasters and the modest RAF navigator in the cricket field. He glanced sideways at Gus, who was still not smoking.

The middle Ainslie girl had red eyes when he last saw her, because the shy navigator was missing after bombing factories at Dresden. John anatomized the Fortress. You could still see the slender lines of the pre-war original, that had been practically unarmed and a sitting duck. They had just altered the tail and stuck guns all over the place . . . It was pretty boring, really. Just a stupid old Flying Fortress.

He heard Gus sniff. Gus was too stupid even to keep his own nose clean. John moved a little to one side, pretending to himself that he must check whether this plane had the latest gun positions on each side of the nose – cheek guns, Pilger said they were called . . .

Gus was rustling a packet.

– And was the rear turret a little different from the latest version . . . ?

John heard a match scrape. That was what he had been waiting for. But of course, even Gus would take care, wouldn't he? And anyway, a match would almost certainly go out in the wet grass . . . He smelt the richness of Virginia flooding the damp air.

'All right then, let's go.' John picked up his bike and straddled it. Not until he shoved off did he see the flame leap where Gus had stood.

'Look out!'

'Wha-at?' Two descending notes of exasperation as, without turning round, Gus urged his bike away.

'There's a fire!'

Gus turned a scared face to where small flames flickered for a moment at the edge of the concrete on which the plane stood. Then there was a low sound – a sort of grunt – and a hot blast of air as the dispersal point was swallowed in a ball of flame just like yesterday's.

'Come on!' They stood on their pedals, and hunched low over the handlebars as they gathered speed. There were no sounds of alarm; probably no one realized that the plane had not been rolled clear. John glanced back at the hut and saw that its door was still closed. He concentrated on pedalling, following Gus's back wheel. At the second group of huts they stopped and looked back. A smear of smoke still hung in the air, but the drab Fortress stood revealed again, apparently unharmed. The fire must have burnt itself out. It had only been a little petrol, after all.

'Phew!' said Gus. 'That put the wind up me.'

They started off again and John, freewheeling, turned to take a last look. He wobbled and nearly fell off at the pounding under his ribs; there was a shimmer of hot air over the starboard wing of the Fortress and – yes – small flames round the engine cowling.

It was important not to panic. He concentrated on following Gus's stupidly innocent back, maintaining a carefree expression as trucks hummed slowly past. They were in sight of the main gate when he heard the thump of the explosion. Gus stopped and looked round. Yanks were looking too. The truck that had just overtaken them ran on in ignorance. John came up to Gus and the two of them looked back to where an expanding mass of incandescence hung in the air. They craned their necks and could see the Fortress, slumped on one wing from which the fire was pouring. Small figures were running out of the hut and cringing at the edge of the dispersal area. But now the whole thing was engulfed in flames, and a few seconds later there came the muffled sound of a second explosion as another fireball elaborated itself.

Fire engines rushed past. 'Come on, you guys. Clear the camp!' an officer shouted at them from a jeep. Grateful at this dismissal they rode out of the gate and down the lane, saying nothing. At least, Gus started to say something, but John pedalled ahead and pretended not to hear.

Finally, Gus came up alongside and insisted: 'That Fortress . . . do you think –'

'It wasn't anything to do with us,' said John. 'We didn't start a fire, did we? – I haven't got any matches.'

Gus was silent.

'Serves the stupid Yanks right – wasting petrol on cleaning planes. They just went off and left it, didn't they? That's asking for trouble.' Gus brooded over his handlebars and John added, without much conviction: 'It was probably the sun on some broken glass.'

'Yeah, that's what I thought,' said Gus.

They parted at the crossroads and John headed back towards Pilger's place. Yesterday his handlebars had been the control column of a Fortress as he rode in close formation with Pilger. Today the real events of the afternoon crowded out imagination until the last stretch before the half-timbered farmhouse. He took that very fast, in a Mosquito running for home at rooftop height, unarmed, but escaping interception by sheer speed.

On the Aberdonian

In the queue at King's Cross I remembered I had to make a telephone call. I did not want to lose my place, but when I wondered aloud about phone booths and looked round despairingly, the man in thick Scotch tweeds who stood next to me twinkled his eyes and cheerfully pouted his grey moustache as he told me to leave my case with him and he would have an eye to it.

'Did ye get through?' he asked, when I returned.

'Afraid not.'

He shook his head sympathetically, then, after a few minutes' consideration he said, in his judiciously crooning, highland voice, 'Pretty good, these fast trains, I believe,' and we exchanged a few more polite banalities, as was appropriate between civilized provincials escaping from the rude metropolitan world.

The train was not full, and I found a window seat just across the carriage gangway from the man in tweeds and his wife. A shy girl – an American, judging from her ritualized courtesy and ready smile – joined them. They welcomed her to the other side of their table, and gently proceeded to interrogate and commend her. I caught snatches of 'Ah, your sister stays in Elgin? Oh, that's nice, that's very nice – you'll be glad to get out of London for a spell . . . ' and 'oh, studying art? Oh good. Well, I can tell you my wife is quite a one for her crafts . . . '

I decided the couple were respected citizens of some tidy, windswept town in the eastern highlands. A schoolmaster and his wife, perhaps. But no, he lacked the stern but distracted eyes of a teacher. A minister, then? Too unguarded. Possibly a shopkeeper, but more likely a retired professional man, or a modest landowner.

At Doncaster more people joined the train, and the quartet of seats round my table received two youths with shoulder-length hair, one with his arm in a sling. They sat down quite politely, one beside me and one opposite, and spoke about high boots and lobster-pots. But they were not weather-beaten enough for fishermen. They were not Scottish, either, and referred to the Scots as 'they', who were pretty wild with those big – what were they called?

'Claymores.'

'Are they made of wood or are they plastic?'

'Iron!' and the bandaged arm was exhibited. 'He made a mess of my lobster-pot, too – why are they called lobster-pots, anyway? Is it the bars in front or is it the joints at the back?'

'Dunno. We just wear morions – like the Swiss Guards.'

I had it. They were members of one of those clubs that re-enact historical battles. I vaguely remembered that those helmets with earflaps such as Cromwell wore were called 'lobster-pots', and I, too, had wondered why.

'Is this seat taken?'

An old lady was asking the uninjured toy soldier, who sat facing me with an empty seat beside him. He smiled, lifted her case on to the rack and made room for her.

'Thank you for your courtesy,' she recited, as she sat down. Then she listened bemusedly to more talk of claymores and pikes and how if you had a good morion you stood to lose it if someone got a pike underneath it, and the problem with boots leaking – because you couldn't choose your ground, you see . . . After ten minutes of that she fetched a copy of *The Lady* out of her bag and read it without glasses, a gentle smile on her still pretty face, where freckles declared she had once been fair-haired. Now her hair was grey and carefully cut short. Her dove-coloured blouse with ornamental stitching round the collar seemed to be of real silk, and she wore good jewellery – more of it than one at first realized.

The two boys got out at York, and the old lady ate as daintily as a cat. Had she been English her foil packet would have contained neatly triangulated sandwiches, but she was Scottish and lunched tidily on halved salad rolls, with coffee from the buffet. At Darlington she smilingly welcomed a lady in a sari to the seat beside her, and the sari lady smiled back complacently when the old lady congratulated her on living in Edinburgh – 'such a centre!' She herself was from Aberdeen, of course, though she was going no further than Dundee today. She did not praise Aberdeen, but she pronounced the name with emphasis and a quiet smile. She really was a charming, bright old lady, with her freckles and the gentle smile that seemed her natural facial expression.

At Newcastle a few people left the train, dragging heavy suitcases, and were replaced by a few others carrying even heavier rucksacks. But an hour later, at the distant sight of Arthur's Seat, half the occupants of the carriage began scrabbling for their luggage. As the train ran into Waverley Station the lady in the sari levered her case-on-wheels into the gangway and chivvied the heels of the people blocking the way, and the highland lady from the seats opposite urged her tweedy husband into the crush.

'We don't stop here but we hope to meet our eldest son,' she explained as she passed. 'He's working in Edinburgh and he'll have come to see us as we go through . . . Oh dear!' and she craned anxiously over the heads of the people in front.

The train stopped and the queue surged forward, pinning rash incomers to the back of the vestibule with their cases between their knees. The highland wife led from behind, her arm already sketching a wave to her son. Suddenly they were all gone. The few incomers entered like shy birds, pecking diffidently at the quartets of seats to find an empty place.

'You know . . .' It was the old lady, leaning across the table and confiding. 'You know, I've taken rather a dislike to that woman over there,' and she indicated the seats, marked with neatly folded coats, where the highland couple had sat. I crooned surprise.

'Well, you see, she misinformed me about the seats. I asked if those two seats were taken and she said this one was but the other wasn't, only I haven't seen anyone sitting in either – and while I was asking, her husband had his coat on this one and he made no effort to move it.'

I became aware of my jacket on the seat beside me.

'Now, I'll say nothing about those two boys who were here

just now. They couldn't have been more helpful. I don't say I really wanted my case up there on the rack, but they were most courteous for all their queer talk, and I'll say nothing about long hair again.'

I agreed about the boys as I slipped on my jacket. The old lady indicated two jugs on the table across the aisle.

'Do you know what they had in those jugs?'

I said I really had no idea.

'That's tea in there,' said the old lady. 'Fancy having tea in jugs! Everyone else had these plastic cups. The whole queue had to stand and wait while the attendant fetched those jugs. He had to hunt in all the cupboards. They kept everybody waiting.'

I hummed disapprovingly.

'Is she Scottish?' asked the old lady.

I said I thought so.

'Well, I don't. I thought I detected a slight accent.' And she leaned back and returned to her copy of *The Lady* as the highland pair came back into the carriage. They were beaming. They had met their son and the wife was proudly holding a new book of poetry.

'That's very nice,' she said, showing it to me. 'It'll give me great pleasure when I get home – it's all my favourite Scottish poets and some new ones I don't know at all. And it's a treat to have a nice book in proper covers nowadays.' She settled down to dip here and there with little exclamations to her husband, who nodded and twinkled his pleasure.

'Excuse me, are there two seats here?' A young man was leaning over me with a bright smile of enquiry. 'Oh, good. I'll fetch the wife and kiddies.'

The anxious wife, carrying a two-year-old, settled surprisingly broad hips into the seat beside me and supervised her husband's struggles with the luggage and the second child. At last he subsided next to the old lady and I saw her glance apprehensively at the predatory babe on his lap. For a moment I wondered if she regretted causing me to clear away my jacket, but she smiled so sweetly at the young wife that the thought seemed unworthy.

The parents were conscientious, but the youngsters were

fretful after what had evidently been a long journey. The old lady kept her eyes steadily on her text, but the highland couple smiled across the aisle at the family, and the man pouted his moustache and tickled one of the children. The mother smirked her approval. Then she supervised the administration of food by her husband, while the highlanders welcomed the return of the American girl (so there *had* been only one seat to spare).

'Have you been lunching yourself?' asked the highland husband. Oh no, she had just fallen asleep up there in first class, she replied, and, unaware of his puzzlement, she fell to admiring the new book that his wife proudly showed her.

Shortly after Cupar passed by, the highland man rose, wiping his dry moustache. Would they like some tea? Oh, yes, they could all drink a cup of tea! So he went off to the buffet to see what he could do. When he had gone his wife whispered something to the American girl.

'There's one that's just fine along there in the first,' came the reply. 'I had a job finding it, though. The one here seems to be out of use – look, why don't I show you?' and they set off with conspiratorial purpose just as the landscape fell away and we lunged out over the grey expanse of the Tay.

I was getting off at Dundee, and so it seemed was nearly everyone. The young couple levered their children into shapeless packages of outer clothing and applied them to pushchairs. The old lady got up and looked at her case and I, eager to show that a beard was no worse than long hair, leaped to fetch it down. In doing so I stood on the foot of the young mother, who was busy doing up straps.

'Do you think you could help me with this, please?' she snapped. The train was running into the station, but I waited until she was satisfied with the arrangement of the child, then helped her get the pushchair to the door and hand it down to her husband, who by this time was on the platform. Knowing that those fast trains don't stop very long, I turned to hurry back for my things and tripped over the other child. I don't think I hurt it much, but I had to make a second, more elaborate, apology to its mother's indignant backside before I could stumble back into the carriage for my coat and bag.

'Oh!' Another cry of pain!

The highland lady had returned from the lavatory. Now she stood aghast in the gangway, then hurried forward to the table where her new book lay open, flooded with the dregs from an overturned mug – which had, I noticed, contained Bovril, not tea. She was so distressed that for a moment I forgot my hurry.

'However did that happen?' she cried

I didn't know. It was certainly none of my doing. And I was still standing there, watching her tender wiping, and trying to think of some consolation, when I realized that the train had started. As it carried me off, an unwilling passenger to Arbroath, I saw the face of the pretty old lady accelerating past the window. Her blue eyes looked intently into the carriage as it passed, and she still wore her sweet smile.

Pleasures of the Flesh

Henry Sturrock had cheeks like a great catch of plankton netted in a tissue of fine crimson veins. Seen in a glancing light their slabby sides had the gloss of uncooked sausages. That was appropriate because Henry, though in many ways a puritan, was fond of eating – of eating anything. He was not concerned with gastronomy, but simply with putting things into his mouth, chewing them – without particular attention to their flavour – and swallowing them to the accompaniment of several pints of tea a day.

Henry lived with his sister Annie, who spent half her time keeping herself, her house, her clothes and Henry's linen spotlessly clean, and the rest in cooking large meals of what Henry called 'plain English fare'. Along with a great deal of sugar and flour, the grocer delivered quantities of scouring powder, double cubes of household soap, a reassuring amount of the less indulgent sort of toilet paper ('more sensible') and a parcel of tea (but no coffee). In an emergency Annie might strain the tolerance of Providence by cooking with butter instead of margarine, but she never exposed her inner self to the alien slipperiness of that horrid olive oil.

Henry and Annie attended church regularly and contributed to charity in the little envelopes that cheerfully porcine Hilda Stubbs brought round each week – she left an empty one and collected another gorged with twenty-five pence. Henry's religion was sincere, but he had never pondered its mysteries and the nearest he had come to enthusiasm had been a spasm of fascinated revulsion at the age of eight.

That had come about because he and Annie had been sent to Sunday school. There, the young women who discoursed on

175

pious themes soon either ran out of material or became too embarrassed by the intimacies of religion to continue. The children were left to look at picture books, and Henry sat in the unfamiliar hall leafing through a folio volume with another unnaturally tidy child. They came across a vivid picture of the crucifixion and gazed at it dutifully.

The other child drew moist fingers over the paper where it bore images of piercing spikes, and wrists and feet tearing under the weight that hung on them. The child hissed its horror and rattled snot in its nose. Henry had often sat in church gazing quite happily at the big east window with its wanly resigned figure on the cross, but he, too, was horrified now. The thorns reminded him of reaching for lost balls under rose bushes, and the spear poking into the side – he shut the book on the other child's hand and went away. Later he returned to refresh his revulsion alone.

But that had been in early childhood. Now Henry again confronted the east window with vacant ease, anticipating lunch but in no danger of imagining the pangs of the stigmata. After church and the joint there was the *Sunday Express,* and sometimes he might give a few minutes to Annie's *News of the World,* always folding it carefully afterwards (for it was not his) and observing that he didn't know what things were coming to. It puzzled him that people could not be content with three meals a day and a job that kept them occupied.

Henry worked for a firm of wholesale seedsmen. He was a conscientious employee and respected by his colleagues as a 'clean-living man'. His speech was as unblemished as his linen. If there was lewd talk his mouth set straight, its ends pinned firmly into the upholstery of his cheeks, and he shook his head as he bent over his desk. He had little time for reflection, but in spare moments he might recapitulate the last meal, or consider the likely composition of the next.

Most things reminded Henry of food. Fields of corn spoke of the heady smell of fresh crusty loaves (though Henry usually clogged his gums with damp sliced bread that Annie regarded as more sensible). The rabbits that peopled the corn suggested cavernous pies, clotted with jelly that relinquished pale, delicately muscled limbs with succulent reluctance. Bullocks

176

exercised steaks before Henry's eyes; cheeses accumulated beneath cows, bacon and ham swelled the hides of pigs. Ducks waited for peas and anticipated with their dabbling the sputter of juices in the pan; lambs dedicated themselves to preparation for a liaison with mint sauce.

Henry, who had never looked at a woman with concupiscent eyes, did review young girls with a literally carnal interest. In the era of mini-skirts the sturdy thighs that flashed between skirt-hem and boot-top in every street suggested roasting joints, nicely trimmed. On Ramsgate sands he confronted tanned expanses of rib and navel, but saw chops and belly bacon. Even the pale legs of paddling Annie reminded him of the goose-pimpled blue-pink limbs of an oven-ready chicken.

Ramsgate was where Henry and Annie shared a bungalow with brother Fred and his family each summer. Each fine day Henry carried the basket of food when they all went down to the beach. After splashing about with the youngsters he enjoyed tea and cucumber sandwiches, then sat gazing out to sea till it was time to go for a fish lunch at one of the restaurants on the front. The last time they went there was one unsettling moment, which only Henry, and possibly Annie, noticed and which neither of them understood.

Sally, the younger of the two nieces, was cavorting about in the sand beside Henry's deck-chair building castles for her little brother. Sally was fifteen or sixteen – Henry had lost track – and growing fast. Her bathing suit, new that season, was already too small and the long, plumpening limbs of incipient womanhood sprouted energetically from the drum-tight fabric that stretched round the circumference of her back. She reminded Henry of a young leveret, skinned for jugging – but neater, like a squirrel, though you can't eat squirrels. Henry felt an unfamiliar sensation and hurriedly heaved himself out of his chair, hitched up his trunks and headed for the water.

'Are you all right, Henry?' asked Annie, anxiously.

'Bit hot – just going for a dip,' said Henry over his shoulder.

'Now, there's a sight in a million,' grinned brother Fred as Henry pounded off. Sally sprinted into the water after him and Henry, recovered, bounced in the waves and tumbled her as he always did.

The summer passed into autumn and the church was heaped with richness and plenty for the harvest festival. Then came Christmas, which Annie and Henry observed conscientiously, with feasting. They had their own turkey, then went to brother Fred's for the rest of the day and plugged any crevices that had opened with ham salad, mince-pies and cake. On Boxing Day the family came to eat Annie's turkey, cold, and to make a good tea. Afterwards the women murmured about fitted washbasins and Linda's young man, who had come for tea and taken her for a walk. Linda was Sally's elder sister. Arthur, the young man, pink and slightly pustular in his blue suit, was the butcher's son. Arthur had told Henry not to worry about the shortage of manure for the garden. 'Just go round to the slaughterhouse,' he advised. 'Get some blood-and-bone meal – that'll do the trick. My dad always uses it.'

Henry was not keen. He wanted the 'real stuff', but all the farmers he knew seemed to have gone intensive and their land had a pungency that Annie would not have tolerated at her back door. Even the Colonel, whose stable had been a standby, was contracted to the mushroom farm. So blood-and-bone it would have to be. After all, Arthur's father's leeks were famous.

Henry drove his Morris round to the slaughterhouse after work. (The board at the gate called it an 'abattoir', now, he noticed.) The day's business was done, but a few men remained, playing hoses and urging floods of soiled water down the drains with wide brooms. They waved Henry 'through to the other side' for his fertilizer. He had never been in a slaughterhouse before. The wet, desolate spaces reminded him of those Monday afternoons when he had come home from school to find his mother still clearing up from washday, with everything bleakly disordered and damp.

There was a rank smell of the faeces voided by frightened beasts. Henry imagined them blundering terrified, even more lost than he was in this awful place that smelt of blood and death. The thousands that had passed through the empty caverns seemed almost more impressive in their absence than they must have been as they stumbled and jostled in wide-eyed droves.

Henry must have taken a wrong turning, for he came to a dead end enclosed by high walls. The drab brickwork, the whitewashed cornerstones, reminded him of army depôts where he had been utterly miserable, and the Victorian solidity of the walls added to the sense of imprisonment. Anxious to get away, Henry went for directions into a tiled place where men were still working. He turned back when he found zinc tubs on wheels, brimming with intestines and – could it be? Yes – sprinkled with staring eyes. As he hurried out past a heap of severed tongues he nearly fell into a cistern of blood.

He was after blood-and-bone meal, so he must be getting warm. No doubt the clanking machine over there and the chimney that projected from a low roof and emitted heavy smoke had something to do with it. Yes, the stuff was round the back – a man with bloody overalls who came to see what Henry wanted confirmed that. 'Fourth bay,' he said. 'You'll find someone there.'

As he made his way 'round the back' Henry's vague sense that this reminded him of something exceptionally horrible increased, but he refused to think about it. Here were the bays. To reach the fourth he had of necessity to pass the other three. The first was stacked with a great heap of hides with tattered, bloody margins. They were quite shapeless now, yet in the awkwardness of their flatness they were eloquent of the warm bulks that had occupied them – until today.

Now Henry knew where he had seen it before – the bleak, half-hygienic buildings, and the awful absence of the many who had been driven to their deaths. He remembered the picture magazines at the barber's in 1945, after the concentration camps had been overrun. The next bay was ghastly with heaps of horns and the third recalled still more vividly the photographs that had horrified the world – including Henry, as he waited for his weekly trim from Curly Sandford. Hooves were piled there like empty shoes; some had traces of earth and even blades of grass still caught between the toes. Henry knew now that he was in an animal Auschwitz, and when he reached the fourth bay the smell of the freshly ground bone, blood and God-knew-what else was sickening as it was shovelled into a filthy sack. Henry tried not to breathe as he carried it out to his car, and retched when he lifted it out at home.

Annie was hurrying out to help get the church hall ready for St Mary's organ-fund social. She afterwards recalled being puzzled by her brother's subdued manner and his lack of enthusiasm for corned beef, but she was in a hurry. As she left she encouraged him to come along later – seeing people might take him out of himself a bit.

Henry did change his suit and walk round to brother Fred's, so they could all go down to the hall together. He found the household bubbling with excitement and Sally jumped around him, proclaiming that Linda and Arthur had become engaged. The two of them were not there – they wanted to be alone together, giggled Fred's wife Babs. Henry waited patiently in his accustomed place; hands clasped behind his back and warming at the imitation coal fire. Everyone smiled conspiratorially as they passed. The whole house seemed to be seething with sexual tension and an expectation that he, the bachelor uncle, would be embarrassed. In fact he was quite unconcerned. He just couldn't get that place out of his mind.

At last Babs pronounced herself ready and they all walked the few steps to the hall together. In the porch they met Maisie Haines from the sub-post office, who crowed at the news and pouted reddened lips to mark Babs's cheek. Then she offered her own face to Fred, who gallantly swept her into his arms. Maisie feigned alarm and rolled her eyes fearfully towards the new curate, beaming fatly in the doorway. Henry looked at the woman and saw the slewed, staring eyeballs of a terrified animal. Then, when Maisie, her eyes now mercifully half-closed, stretched her neck forward and offered her face to him, he recalled the tubs of pink offal and smelt the reek of blood-and-bone meal in her powerful scent.

Henry went into the hall, smiling and nodding to people he knew, pulling himself together and banishing the thought that they were all walking animal cemeteries. He took a sandwich from a proffered dish, but when he found the cucumber was embedded in a paste that could have been made from that stuff, he covertly dropped it on to an unattended plate. He exchanged commonplaces with gardening cronies about the cold snap and whether there was any point in getting seed into the ground.

Then the curate got the gramophone playing and started to organize games. Henry, excused by age, retired behind some palms and reflected that he was not himself at all. That place had really upset him.

'Come on Uncle Henry, you can play musical chairs!' It was Sally. Henry smiled and reluctantly let her lead him out to join the self-conscious circle shuffling round the row of chairs. Henry tripped to 'Shepherds' Hey' and when the music stopped he nearly descended on Hilda Stubbs's lap, but managed to divert his fall to the chair beside her. Hilda flashed a chubby grin at him before the music started again. Henry resolved that he would contrive to be out next time, and was glad to see the curate whisking chairs away with heavy joviality.

'Now then,' cried the curate. 'It's going to musical laps from now on. Gentlemen in the chairs please. Come on Mr Instep – here you are, Mr Sturrock!' And Henry found himself thrust into a chair. The curate set the gramophone going again, and the women circled. Then there was a great slithering scramble when the music stopped. Henry saw Hilda Stubbs's trotters skidding on the parquet as if it were wet concrete. Then he received Maisie's rump in a rolling bovine flop. He smiled falsely at her beaming eye, saw at close range its bloody suffusion and hurriedly looked away. He refused to brood on the fact that, moribund himself, he was nursing another potential cadaver.

The music started again. Maisie gathered her sprawled limbs and, her bony hinquarters grinding and surging on his lap, hauled herself to her feet. The jolly curate tapped Henry on the shoulder in merciful dismissal.

Henry lingered politely for a moment or two, watching the women sidle round the men, darting their hips in false starts at every other step. Then, as Maisie crashed with a scream of triumph on to the avid loins of grinning old Charlie Instep, Henry made for his retreat behind the palms. But there were people already there, so he settled for a chair on the near side of the greenery. The music had started again and he waved and smiled as Maisie fluttered heifer's eyelashes and Hilda flourished a forehock. He looked the other way and saw that the people on the far side of the palms and ferns were Linda and

Arthur. They were talking, leaning to each other, heads bowed in apparent contemplation of the two pairs of hands that were clasped before them. Now they slid into a fervent embrace.

Fascinated, Henry watched Linda's thrusting knee and Arthur's clutching hand. He could hardly believe that this was the creature he had dandled a few years before. He observed how Linda's eyes were closed as if in prayer; Arthur's were not quite shut, but his profile expressed the extreme absorption of a dog at its dinner. Henry was surprised to see that the two mouths appeared to be open and the jaws were working spasmodically. In shocked understanding he imagined an insidious intrusion in his own mouth and recalled the heaped tongues with their severed roots on the slaughterhouse tiles.

'Uncle, you're peeping!' cried Sally as she pounced. Henry felt himself blush as he confronted the teasing face. The blue irises danced in clear whites, the laughing teeth were set in pink gums – it seemed the epitome of gaiety and health. But Henry saw it sliced apart for veal – he supposed calves' faces went into veal and ham pies . . . .

Sally giggled and suddenly kissed him on the cheek. 'There!' she said. 'So you aren't left out!'

Henry could not understand any of it. Poor Maisie had become a walking corpse, Linda had turned him into an obsessed Peeping Tom, and now young Sally had flooded him with unhappiness just because she was so thoughtlessly and vulnerably young – and that was somehow connected with the time she had squirmed in the sand at Ramsgate. Henry avoided the laughing face, turning his eyes towards the end wall which, since this was a church hall, was made pious with stained glass. But Henry saw in the bland Victorian crucifixion the agony of the tortured animal in the Sunday school picturebook and hurriedly turned away again.

Maisie was talking and grinning with all her teeth. Charlie Instep was looking hungrily at Hilda Stubbs's buttocky breasts as they crowded the top of her blouse. Now Maisie popped a sandwich into her mouth to feed the body that slewed wearily under her flowery dress and Charlie, leaning back to laugh, bared his false teeth and let his belly sag over his belt.

Suddenly Henry wanted the world swept clean of all this

decadent flesh and repopulated with fresh, untainted bodies. Gently he shoved Sally aside as he stood up. Then he bolted across the room. Charlie Instep, who got in the way, was nearly knocked down. Annie looked up anxiously from her tea urn. People stopped in their tracks as Henry galloped past. He rushed into the gents' lavatory, slammed the door and leaned wearily on the washbasin, staring in the mirror.

An ill-shaven, broken-veined, bleary-eyed face looked back at him. Animals were killed long before they reached this state – while they were in the prime of life, like Sally. He loathed his decaying chops. There came a knocking at the door and Fred's embarrassed enquiry. Annie's voice was in the background, saying he must have eaten something. Henry leaned on the washbasin, flexed his arms, flung back his head and let out a great howl.